The Fixing Tree

By

Rayford E. Hammond

The Fixing Tree

Rayford E. Hammond

Chapter 1

A thick layer of fog blanketed the valley below and crept silently upward across the bluff, silhouetting the naked, winter-bare oak, poplar and hickory trees growing along the brow. Billowy white cotton-like wisps meandered around the boulders forming the edge of the bluff, then slithered stealthily across the backyard, causing visibility to deteriorate to the point that the gray squirrels were becoming nearly invisible and ghostlike as they scampered up and down the trunks of the huge, 100-yr-old trees. Even the few red cardinals hopping around in the yard appeared dull and gray in the dank atmosphere, affording a scene reminiscent of the kind produced in a charcoal drawing. Only the fleeting movement of these few squirrels and birds, along with an occasional wandering neighborhood dog, interrupted the otherwise eerie stillness. As the fog surrounded the small house that backed onto the bluff, the reduced visibility seemed to carry with it a kind of mysterious, unsettling silence.

Glancing out my window to the south, I could barely make out a silhouette of the old Wilson house on the lot bordering my property. I often wished that house were farther away than the couple of hundred feet separating our two properties, particularly when the old lady's numerous dogs took to barking—and I had concluded that it didn't take much to excite them into action. I smiled, remembering the

2 *RAYFORD E. HAMMOND*

admonitions by some of the mountain folk about the crazy old woman who lived next door, along with her horde of dogs and cats. From the few times I had seen or spoken with the old lady, I had to agree that, although she appeared harmless, her *elevator might not go all the way to the top floor.* She was prone to wander about, both day and night, and I frequently saw her walking along East Brow Lane, the country road providing access to the few houses along the bluff. Sometimes she walked through people's yards, usually with her head down and seemingly in a daze, with three or four dogs trailing along behind, and usually a cat or two cradled in her arms.

During the few months I had lived here on the mountain, the old woman had appeared at my door twice: once at seven o'clock in the morning, ostensibly to apologize for her barking dogs having disturbed me. Realizing she was probably just lonely, I hadn't had the heart to tell her it was her ringing of my doorbell, not the barking dogs, that had awakened me. Another time she came over complaining about having lost her flashlight. She asked if I would mind picking up a new one for her the next time I went down the mountain into town. I bought her a new flashlight that same day, but later when I tried to give it to her, she seemed to have forgotten about asking for it and couldn't understand why I was offering her a new flashlight. After much pleading for her to take the flashlight as a gift, she finally agreed. Later that evening, I noticed her walking down the road, shining the new flashlight from side to side.

The lonesome wail of a train whistle wafted upward from the valley floor, barely penetrating the floor-to-ceiling, double-insulated windows across the back of my house, gently rousing me from my reverie. Were it not for the fog, I could have seen the toy-like freight train slowly snaking its way along the valley floor far below. I could almost hear the clanging of the rails as the long chain of boxcars rumbled along, reminding me of the several trains that once passed daily through the little town. As a boy, I had frequently counted the boxcars, which on the freight trains often numbered more than a hundred. I remembered how excited I would become when finally I saw the little red caboose approaching. I would wave at the men in the striped coveralls manning the engine and the caboose, and they would wave back. But it was the passenger trains that had fascinated me most. These usually consisted of twelve or fifteen coaches filled with laughing, well-dressed people. I would wave to them, wondering where they were going and wishing I too could be traveling to some exciting, faraway place. Now, only a few lone freight trains traveled the dying rails, making their appearance once or twice weekly, the wail of their whistle proclaiming a slow death of the railway, and perhaps also of the little town.

Glancing out the window to the north, I noticed the fog was so thick now that I could barely see the skeleton of the new house under construction on the lot bordering my property on that side. The house appeared about half finished, but construction had slowed when winter set in. I had not met the young couple who were having the house built, but had heard they were coming from Johnson City, Tennessee, just across the state line to the north. It seemed that more and more people from out of the area were discovering the peacefulness and solitude of these mountains.

Suddenly a fleeting shadow caught my eye through the window to my left, next to the outside door. At first I thought it was one of the neighborhood dogs scavenging for a scrap of food, but that conclusion quickly proved false when I heard a woman yelling and banging on my storm door, rattling it so hard that I was afraid the glass might shatter. No doubt, this was the crazy old lady from next door. What could *she* want now?

Something seemed terribly wrong, so I jumped up and hurried toward the door, before she broke the glass and cut herself. "Carter! Carter!" the old lady screamed as she banged on the door. She always called me *Carter*, apparently convinced that was my first name, although I had told her more than once that my name was Tom Carter. I jerked open the door, revealing a bedraggled old woman, dressed in a faded yellow cotton nightgown and cloth house slippers, although the temperature outside could not have been more than 35 degrees. Her eyes were wild and piercing, and her hair, which was almost the color of the fog, lay plastered against her head on one side and stuck straight out like ruffled broom straws on the other.

"Yes, uh. . .come in, Mrs. Wilson. You must be freezing out there."

The old lady continued to stand on the stoop, shivering. She began mumbling breathlessly, "Not gonna die. . .I seen it all. . .not gonna die. . ."

"What? What are you talking about, Mrs. Wilson. Come on in out of the cold. What do you mean? Has something happened to one of your animals, or what?"

The old lady made no movement to come inside. Gasping, she kept repeating the words, "Not gonna die. . .I seen it. . .not gonna die."

I couldn't imagine what the old lady could possibly be talking about as she continued to ramble these nearly unintelligible phrases. At first she seemed terribly upset, but as I stood there speechless, her ramblings became softer and her weathered face began to take on an almost angelic-like appearance. Gasping, as if she were running out of breath with every phrase, she slowly kept repeating, in a raspy voice, "Not gonna die. . .I know these things. . .not gonna die. . .I seen it."

Finally, after apparently exhausting her final breath, she simply stopped speaking. Then slowly she turned and ambled away. I called after her but she didn't look back as she headed across the yard toward her house, disappearing into the fog as suddenly as she had appeared.

"What the..." I wondered aloud as I closed the door and slumped into the recliner beside my desk. What was this crazy old lady talking about? Did she need help with something over at her house, perhaps having to do with one of her cats or dogs? She hadn't seemed to want me to come with her, though. Still, something was obviously wrong, although I couldn't imagine what it might be. Maybe she was just having one of her crazy spells wherein she had trouble separating illusion from reality.

As I got on with my morning activities, I continued to wonder if I ought to go over there and see about her; yet strangely, she seemed to have calmed down before she left, almost as if now that she had conveyed her message to me—whatever it might mean—everything was all right again.

Chapter 2

Patty Carter exhaled in relief, unconsciously running her fingers through her long blond hair, as she slowed the blue Dodge Caravan and prepared to exit the freeway onto the highway leading into the small town of Roan Creek. Both the traffic and the weather had been horrendous during her entire drive, but fortunately she was now only a few miles from her destination. Looking up toward the mountains, she could see only the vast whiteness of the fog.

Patty had been to see her father only once since he moved here, but she remembered having been to Roan Creek several times as a little girl while visiting her grandparents, although they had lived in the valley then. From her previous visit to her father's house on the mountaintop, she recalled the narrow winding road that, even under normal conditions, required one to pay strict attention to driving. In this fog, she imagined it would be even more treacherous.

Patty loved her father dearly, although they didn't always agree on how she should be living her life. *Seldom agreed* might be a better term, she had to admit. Jenny, her seven-year-old daughter, was of course convinced that her Ole Pa hung the stars and the moon, and that he was primarily responsible for the daily rising and setting of the sun. Patty had once felt the same way about him, long ago when she was a little girl. To be honest, even now she still felt it to some extent—wanted to believe it, perhaps—although she could seldom ever admit it, even to herself—and certainly never to him.

Jenny had called her grandfather *Ole Pa* ever since she started talking. Patty often wondered if she should have encouraged her daughter to call him *Pa-Pa*, or something other than *Ole Pa*, fearing this name might continually remind Jenny that she had an *Old Pa* but not a *Young Pa*. The name had stuck, though, and it was too late now to change it. *Ole Pa's not actually all that old,* Patty reminded herself. She had been born when he was only twenty-one and they frequently joked that they had grown up together. She had to admit, though, that he had grown up a lot more than she had. Still, he wasn't old. He had always looked and acted years younger than his chronological age, which was. . .she had to stop and think for a moment. . .fifty-eight, this year. Could that be right? Even so, he was *not* old.

Patty was looking forward to seeing her father, although she wished the visit could be under better circumstances. No doubt he would feel obliged to express his opinion about her *rash* decision, as he would call it. And he would of course be correct. She didn't want to argue with him about that, though. There was no way she was going to stay with that man—when had she started calling him *that man*—for even one more day. Not after what Jenny had told her yesterday. She couldn't believe the man she had lived with for nearly a year could possibly have done anything like that; yet, neither could she discount her daughter's account of what had happened.

Patty hated to take Jenny out of school in the middle of the year, and worried about what she was going to do about that. There had been no choice, though; she had to leave, and she had to leave today. She had not confronted *him* with the allegation; she had waited until he was away on a job and had simply left, without telling him where she was going. Maybe he wouldn't figure out where she had gone, since she didn't think he knew her father's address, and the phone number was unlisted. Probably he would never try to get in touch with her again anyway. If even a portion of what Jenny had said was true, then he must know that he was liable for arrest. No, Kirby probably wouldn't try to locate her, Patty concluded, and even if he did, she should be able to dispose with him forthwith. Of course, if her father found out about what had allegedly happened, he would want to kill the man; he had never liked Kirby anyway. Patty was beginning to wonder now what she had ever seen in that man— perhaps some false sense of security or stability? But their relationship had been anything but stable. Still, although Jenny did not normally lie, Patty had difficulty believing that Kirby could have done the things Jenny had told her.

In retrospect, Patty wished she had kept her job at the credit union, although it had been a dead-end position for quite some time. Her recent decision to quit the job and help her *significant other* with his new business of selling and installing aluminum siding had so tied Patty to the man, particularly financially, that once she left him, she had no immediate means of support. With hardly any money in savings and with no job or income, she couldn't even afford to rent an apartment. She could have gotten another job, of course, but the kind of work she might have obtained quickly would have been like all her other jobs: dead-end, minimum wage and boring.

Patty had always wanted to teach, and still regretted not having gotten her teaching certificate back when it would have been relatively easy. Now, she would have to take additional college courses and complete her student teaching, which seemed too hard, with her involved in making a living and raising a daughter. Without even enough money to acquire a new place to live, she certainly couldn't consider preparing for a new career at this stage of her life. She had seen no choice but to call her father and ask him if she and Jenny could come and stay with him for a while, at least until she figured out what she was going to do with her life.

As she approached the first turn where the highway started its long ascent up the side of Roan Mountain, Patty remembered that the road ran at an angle, first in one direction and then another. The portion of road she was on now headed generally in a northerly direction up the side of the mountain, until coming to a curve that her father called a *horseshoe turn*, after which the road angled back in the other direction for another mile or so. Following a second horseshoe turn, the highway again angled up the mountain in a northerly direction for the last leg. At the top, it took a ninety-degree turn through a gap in the bluff, and a few hundred yards beyond this gap was the turn to her father's house, which was actually just a narrow country lane leading to the few houses along the bluff.

Patty was tired, frustrated and beyond ready to be there. Jenny had been a pain for the past hour, complaining about one thing or another and continually asking typical seven-year-old traveler's questions: "Are we there yet?" or "How much farther is it to Ole Pa's house?" Was it Patty's imagination, or was Jenny different today, somehow more withdrawn? She had gotten terribly excited when Patty had told her they were going to Ole Pa's for a few days, but throughout the trip, Jenny had seemed almost indifferent.

Although she had at last escaped the awful traffic, Patty now found herself on the winding mountain road, with fog so thick she had to concentrate with all her being just to keep the car in the road. Visibility had become nearly nonexistent and Patty could see only a few yards ahead of her. She had slowed to a crawl, straining to see the yellow line in the center of the road.

"Mommy, when are we gonna be there? I'm hungry. Can we stop at McDonalds?"

Patty glanced over at her daughter and frowned. "Sweetie, we ate less than an hour ago. Besides, we've already passed McDonalds."

"But Mommy—"

"Jenny, please! We'll be at Ole Pa's in just a few minutes. Can't you find something to do? Mommy has to concentrate on driving."

Preoccupied with ensuring that she did not miss a turn on the winding road, Patty didn't say anything when out of the corner of her eye she noticed Jenny unfastening her seat belt and reaching into the back seat for her Barbie case. Perhaps that would keep Jenny occupied for the remaining few minutes, Patty rationalized.

Earlier, Patty had located an Asheville radio station, which for the past several minutes had been playing songs from movie musicals, Jenny's favorite kind of music. On the radio now, Maria began singing a song from *The Sound of Music*: "Raindrops on roses, and whiskers on kittens. . ." This reminded Patty that Jenny had been begging for a kitten, which Patty of course had to forbid because *he* hated cats. Ole Pa wasn't exactly fond of them either, but Patty knew that if Jenny asked her grandfather, he would gladly let her have one. Maybe that would help ease the burden of Jenny having to leave her school and her friends.

Jenny was sitting quietly in the front seat now playing with her Barbie dolls. As Patty executed the second horseshoe turn and headed up the final leg toward the top of the mountain, she glanced briefly at her daughter and smiled as the little blond-haired girl mouthed the words along with Maria: ". . .brown paper packages tied up with strings, these are a few of my favorite things." Because of her two missing front teeth, she had trouble pronouncing some of the words; strings came out as *thrings;* favorite sounded like *tha-tho-rite.*

Just as she was about to remind Jenny to fasten her seat belt, Patty glimpsed through the fog what appeared to be the shadow of an oncoming vehicle. Suddenly realizing it was on her side of the road, coming directly toward her, she instinctively slammed on the brakes and swerved to the right. Tires squealed and Jenny screamed as the sudden turn nearly threw the little girl out of her seat. The realization flashed through Patty's mind that Jenny was not wearing her seatbelt, but it was too late now to worry about that.

Suddenly Patty realized that her car was leaving the road. Because of the fog, she couldn't tell if there was a guardrail along this stretch of the highway; neither could she determine the severeness of the drop-off to her right. Her mind processing at warp speed, she realized that in an instant she must decide which would be worse—hitting the oncoming vehicle head-on, or running off the bluff.

Chapter 3

Getting up from my recliner, I walked into the bathroom. *Gotta cut down on the coffee*, I mused. While washing my hands, I glanced at my image in the mirror. Instead of drying my hands on the towel, I ran them through my wiry brown hair, then absentmindedly took a comb from the medicine cabinet and began pulling it through my thick, tousled hair. For years my hair had been graying around the temples, but I had noticed recently that specks of gray were beginning to appear throughout.

Staring back into my dark blue eyes reflecting from the mirror, I ran my hand across my face, realizing I had neglected to shave this morning. *Must be getting lazy in my old age.* I took my electric razor and made a few quick passes across my face. My heavy beard was also becoming grayer now, too, rendering the five-o'clock shadow less noticeable than it had once been back when I had often been required to shave twice a day. I glanced at my rumpled sweatshirt, the same one I usually wore around the house, and considered whether to change before Patty and Jenny arrived. *Why bother*, I quickly concluded. For some reason, I imagined I could write better when dressed in old jeans and a sweatshirt; but of course, even that hadn't helped recently. I had read somewhere that John Grisham, one of my favorite authors, only shaved once a week when he was writing. I had actually tried that technique myself, but that hadn't helped either.

Again, I noticed I was beginning to suffer from what some called *middle-aged spread*. I sucked in my stomach and held my head high, imagining I still looked pretty good for an old man. Although not so handsome that I received second looks from the ladies, I knew that if he chose, I could still attract a female or two—albeit ones nearer my own age, rather than the younger women to whom I was usually attracted. I smiled, fantasizing that even some of them might still find me attractive.

Probably I should make some effort to meet a nice woman. Since Margie's death, I had avoided any serious involvement, although before moving here, I'd had some offers. Sarah, my sole woman friend here—*acquaintance* might be a better term— had been a year behind me in school. We'd had a casual date or two in high school, but had neither seen each other nor communicated through the years. I had rarely thought of her until a few weeks ago when I encountered her while picking up a few supplies in one of the little town's two supermarkets.

As I was meandering down the produce aisle, I heard a woman calling my name. "Tom? Tom Carter! Is that really you?"

Looking up, I noticed an attractive, gray-haired, middle-aged woman approaching. I didn't recognize her, but quickly realized that I should. She looked vaguely familiar; yet in the instant afforded me to recall her name, I came up blank. Attempting to prevent an embarrassed, questioning look from appearing on my face, I raised my eyebrows, cocked my head and smiled shyly, while trying desperately to think of her name and something appropriate to say. Instead, I muttered the first mundane thing that came to mind. "Last time I checked, it was *really* me."

She stopped a few feet in front of me, smiled coyly and began shaking her head. That smile—it looked so familiar; I should know this woman. One of the problems I had encountered since moving back here was that whenever I went someplace in town, such as to the local supermarket, I often ran across someone who recognized me. They would frequently call me by name, and although I might recognize that I had once known the person, rarely could I remember their name. At first, some of these people had looked to me like the parents of people I had once known here, but soon I concluded that they had simply gotten old while I was away. Could it be that they saw me in the same way? Running into people who recognized me but whose name I could not recall placed me in an awkward and embarrassing position, so I normally avoiding shopping in the little town. Instead, I bought most of my supplies in Asheville, where there was little chance I would encounter anyone I'd once known— although it had also happened there, more than once.

"You don't remember me, do you?"

"Uh . . ."

"Remember the drive-in! That movie, *Splendor in the Grass*! You took me to see that movie—it was my first drive-in experience. Don't you remember? We double-dated with Chuck and Diane. Shame on you, Tom Carter. I guess now I know how much that meant to you."

"Sarah! Sarah Hartman? I'm so sorry—of course, I remember." I struck my forehead with the palm of my hand. "Guess my mind was somewhere else. I just didn't expect to see. . .I mean, it's been so long since . . ."

She took a step toward me and I walked around my shopping cart, extending my hand. She took it and we stood for a moment, then leaned into an awkward half-hug. Backing away, she said, "Actually, it's Sarah *Wallace* now. I haven't been Sarah Hartman for over thirty-five years."

"Yes, of course, I'm sorry. I knew you and John got married, but I'd forgotten. How's he doing?"

Sarah bit her lower lip and looked down. "John died four years ago, Tom—lung cancer. He was sick for a long time before that and couldn't work."

I shook my head. "I'm so sorry, Sarah. I didn't know. That must've been difficult for you." I never knew how to respond to these type situations. *Of course it had been difficult for her!* Why did I always come out with such inane, unthinking statements?

"Yes, these things always are," she said, smiling weakly. "But I've gone on. What choice do we have?"

"Yes, what choice?" I stared across the produce aisle. "I guess only someone who's been through this could ever understand," I finally said.

"That's so true. People always say things like 'I know how you feel', but of course, they don't—how could they?"

"Yeah, how could they? I'm sure they mean well, though." I considered whether to tell her about Margie, but quickly decided against it, feeling that it might come across as some sort of *one-upmanship* tactic.

"Yes, I'm sure they do. The worst is when they say something like 'So, how're you doing, Sarah?' to which I usually reply something like, 'Oh, I'm doing okay, thanks,' to which they sometimes reply 'No, I mean how are you *really doing?*' I just want to say something like, 'Well, how the hell do you think I'm *really* doing. If you *really* want to know, it'll probably take a few hours."

"Right! It's sometimes hard to remember that these people mean well, isn't it? They just don't know what to say, I guess—particularly if they've never had a similar experience."

"I know. I think just letting someone know you're there for them, and that you care, is all that's necessary. Beyond that, you don't have to say anything at all. Certainly, you can't know how someone else feels, so why try to tell them you do?"

"Yeah, that's for sure," I agreed, again finding myself staring across the produce, avoiding looking her in the eye, for reasons I couldn't comprehend.

After a few moments of embarrassing silence, I asked, "So, what are you doing now, Sarah? Didn't you teach for a while some years ago?"

"Yes, and I've been teaching Biology at the high school now for the last three years," she replied, seemingly relieved I had changed the subject. "I had taught some years ago, but then after Cindy came along, I played stay-at-home mom for several years.

Cindy's married now and living in Asheville. I have a beautiful six-year old granddaughter, Tom. Can you believe it?"

"Got ya beat! I have a seven-year old granddaughter—actually, she's nearly eight. Sometime we'll have to exchange pictures. Isn't that what we doting grandparents are supposed to do?"

She smiled and nodded. "Yes, let's do that. By the way, how is Marjorie? I haven't seen her since y'all graduated and she went away to college."

"She, uh. . .Margie passed away a few years ago, Sarah."

"Oh, Tom, I'm so sorry. There I was babbling about my grief and you must've been thinking about that all along."

"It's okay, Sarah. We find a way to go on, don't we?"

"Yes, we don't have much choice, I guess. I'm so sorry, Tom. Now I know you really do understand. . .as only someone who has experienced this sort of thing ever could."

"So true."

Another awkward silence followed during which it seemed neither of us could think of anything appropriate to say. Then we both began speaking at once, talking about how good it was to run each other, which resulted in a good laugh and broke the tension.

"I guess I had an unfair advantage, Tom. I heard you'd moved back here, so I sort of expected I might run into you sometime—and I'm so glad I did. You're living out on the mountain now, right?"

"Yes, in Mother's old house. I've fixed it up, added a room across the back. It's peaceful out there."

"Yes, it is. So, what're you doing with yourself nowadays?"

"Well, I guess you could say I'm sort of retired. I do have a project I've been trying to work on. . .but not very successfully."

"Well, I'd like to hear about that sometime." She glanced at her watch. "But right now I've got to go. I'm supposed to be at a meeting at the school in fifteen minutes—science fair, you remember those don't you? Maybe we could, uh, meet for coffee or something sometime and catch up on old times."

"Yes, I'd like that, Sarah."

"I'm in the phone book—but remember it's Wallace, not Hartman."

"Right. I'll call you soon. It was really good to see you, Sarah. Let's do get together soon."

Twice since that chance occurrence, Sarah and I had met for coffee, and once we'd had lunch together. After a short period of adjustment, we seemed to feel comfortable with one another. But still, I wasn't sure where, if anywhere, the relationship was going. I had recently been thinking of working up to asking her to dinner, but wasn't sure if I wanted our relationship to escalate to that stage just yet.

A few months ago I had decided, much against the wishes of my daughter, to move away from my adopted city of Knoxville, Tennessee, where I had lived since retiring from the navy nearly fifteen years previously. Although I had no family still living in the mountains of North Carolina where I had grown up, and I hadn't kept in close touch with anyone there, I still felt some inexplicable connection to the region. It seemed as if some unknown force urged me back to the land of my roots, as if the spirit of the mountains still lived within me, communicating with my soul, even after all these years. Just driving around the little town of Roan Creek, where I had lived all my life until I'd gone into the navy right after high school, still elicited vivid memories of so many events that had transpired there during my boyhood. Most were good memories, although I had to admit that some were not so good. Still, after all these years, I often felt that the old adage *even the bad times were good* applied in this case. Sometimes my memories of those days were so clear that I felt the events had transpired only last year—or certainly no more than a few years ago. At other times, it seemed they had happened to another person in a different lifetime.

Soon after my wife, Margie, died of a stroke a little more than three years ago, I had gone through the motions of trying to get on with my life. Yet, without my lifelong companion, hardly anything seemed meaningful anymore. I felt I needed a change of pace, and although moving back to the town of my childhood seemed in some respects rather foolish, I could not shake the notion that this was what I was meant to do—where I was destined to spend the remaining years of my life. Although I regretted having to leave my only daughter and granddaughter, I had packed up my things a few months ago and moved into the house I had inherited nearly eight years ago when my mother died.

I had helped my mother purchase the small 3-bedroom ranch house on Roan Mountain shortly after my father died of lung cancer in 1976, at nearly the same age I am now—a fact that sometimes bothered me a lot. Although I had visited my mother here several times, until a few months ago I had never actually lived in this house. Last year when I got the crazy notion that I might want to move back here, I began having the place fixed up, including a new roof, new carpeting, paint, light fixtures and modern plumbing. Of all the renovations, though, my favorite was the expansive windowed room I had added across the back, facing the bluff and overlooking the little town where I had grown up. I spent most of my time in this room now, usually sitting at my computer while endeavoring to accomplish the one purpose I so frequently rationalized was my real reason for moving back here.

Although practically isolated from the rest of the world here in his mountain retreat atop Roan Mountain, I enjoyed the solitude, away from the hustle and bustle to which I had become so accustomed in my previous life. Sometimes the phone did not ring even once throughout the day, and seldom did anyone come to visit, which was just fine with me—or so I rationalized. I often felt stressed now when forced to venture into the fast-paced world of constant data input, even if only for a short time. When away for more than a few hours,

I yearned to be back in my world of seclusion. With access to email and the Internet, along with the ability to be in Asheville, a city of some size, within little more than half an hour, I remained happy with my choice of lifestyle. Here in the mountains, I should certainly have the privacy and peacefulness—perhaps even the inspiration—I felt were necessary to write the novel I had for so long dreamed of completing. The only problem was, after being here for several weeks, all I had been able to produce so far were a few *not-so-good* paragraphs, and it seemed now that I might never be able to proceed past the first chapter.

Five years ago, I had taken up fiction writing, primarily as a means of passing the time after retiring from my second career as a software development engineer. Different from anything I had ever done, the creative venture proved exciting and I quickly discovered that I enjoyed it immensely. Writing became therapeutic, particularly after Margie passed away, and I became so absorbed with the undertaking that I had produced four novels during a three-year period. One of my books had even been published, although the small publisher filed for bankruptcy a few months after releasing the title and I never received any royalties from the work. A couple of other books were now making their way through the snail-like publishing pipeline, but I was afraid to expect much from them. *Don't give up your day job*, as they say. Fortunately, I didn't require nor desire any income from the books in order to survive, particularly living here in the Appalachians where the cost of living was about a fourth of that to which I had been accustomed—even less now, since I had no house payments, no car payments, and no commuting expenses.

Although I considered my earlier novels good, I knew they were not great, and I still maintained my dream of writing a notable book someday. Although it would probably never qualify as the *Great American Novel*, such as my two favorites: "To Kill a Mockingbird" and "Gone With the Wind," for some reason I felt that my best work was yet to be written. At least I had thought this to be true, until struggling for the past several weeks and producing practically nothing. I had begun to wonder if there might not be another book within me at all.

Still, I struggled to finish the first chapter of what I hoped might become my great novel, and every day I sat in front of the computer, typing words that were just that: *words*—meaningless, mundane, and detached. The problem seemed to be that I wasn't able to develop a passion for the story I was trying to develop. No doubt I was trying to force it, which of course never worked. When I had been writing the other novels, there were times when I felt *in the groove*, ideas flowing through me almost as if I were merely a channel. When in this mode, I didn't want to stop, even to eat or go to the bathroom, fearing I would lose that elusive edge. When I did have to leave the computer, I could hardly wait to get back and see what my characters were going to do next, a phenomenon I could never explain to my non-writer friends. Often even the ringing of the telephone would break my train of thought, and sometimes I never got it back. Since moving here, I had not yet achieved this nearly indescribably state, where my fingers raced across the keyboard, producing the story that my characters chose to live, often doing things vastly different from what I had intended them to do. This seemed strange, because here there were few interruptions and I could write 24-hours a day, if I so chose. Still, it just wasn't happening, for whatever reason.

Every day I stared at my computer screen, waiting for some unknown force to possess my fingers and once more send them gliding across the keyboard, producing at blazing speed the poignant story that would quickly become my bestseller. This wasn't happening, though, and hadn't for a long time. I kept looking out the window into the thickening fog, which I concluded must somehow be making its way into my mind. Either I had a story to tell or I didn't; there was no way to force it. I had often heard the term *writer's block*, but never believed in it, thinking that was just the lazy writer's way of making excuses. Now, I wasn't so sure.

Of course, the phone call I had received earlier this morning from my thirty-four year old daughter, Patty, would likely require me to postpone the writing, at least for a while. I had tried to talk her into waiting until tomorrow to commence the trip, as the weather report predicted icy and foggy conditions in the mountains, but Patty had been adamant that she and seven-year-old Jenny were on their way. I expected that if they didn't run into too much adverse weather, they should arrive within the hour, and I could not relax until he knew they were safe. I was aware that Patty and her latest man friend had been having troubles, but hadn't known it had gotten this bad. I often wondered how she had put up with that idiot for so long, and wasn't disappointed that she was finally leaving him.

Naturally, I quickly agreed when Patty asked if she and Jenny could come and stay with me until Patty could get her life back on track. She had sounded desperate and agitated—perhaps even a little frightened—causing me to feel apprehensive already about how this might all work out. Patty certainly had had her troubles with men since the death of Jenny's father six years ago in an automobile accident. In my opinion, she had picked some real *losers*; but from my point of view, this last one seemed the worst, and I could not be unhappy that the man would no longer be playing surrogate father to my only granddaughter. I would, of course, be required to fulfill that role now, at least for a while, and although my granddaughter, Jenny, and I had always been extremely close, I wondered if I was up to the challenge, particularly at my age and stage of life.

I thought frequently about why Patty picked the men she did. Except for Jenny's father, most of her choices had turned out to be mistakes. I was aware of the research and statistics showing that women who had experienced undesirable relationships with their own fathers often picked men who would duplicate that relationship. I was never sure if I believed this, and at least in this one instance, I thought the reason must lie elsewhere. For the most part, Patty and I had a wonderfully close relationship, with our primary recent differences of opinion nearly always relating to her choice of male companions. Of course, given the trauma Patty had gone through when Jenny's father was killed, perhaps there was adequate reason for her downward spiral regarding her relationships.

Walking from the bathroom, I passed through the living room and, as usual, looked at my granddaughter's picture hanging prominently on the wall. I stopped and smiled. The little blond-haired, blue-eyed beauty with her coquettish smile and constant zest for life reminded me so much of Patty when she was that age. Patty told me recently that Jenny had lost her two front teeth since I last saw her, and I tried to imagine what she might look like now. Probably even cuter, I surmised, trying to remember how Patty had looked when she lost her front teeth. Funny, I couldn't seem to recall. Maybe I could find a picture of her taken when she was about Jenny's age. No doubt, my granddaughter would love to see that.

I still marveled that my daughter and granddaughter were so strikingly beautiful. Naturally, they got their good looks mostly from Margie, I realized, but still I allowed himself to feel some small amount of pride. Although Jenny was physically an attractive little girl, I considered that my granddaughter's beauty came primarily from within. Even at age seven she seemed to possess an inner strength and beauty well beyond her years. Perhaps I was simply exercising my rights as a doting old grandpa, though; no doubt, everyone's grandchildren seemed special and exceedingly attractive in their eyes.

Thinking again of Patty, I wondered if I would ever get used to or agree with this new way of thinking among the younger generation regarding marriage and family. It seemed to me that without the commitment of marriage, families were just not what they once were. It didn't bother me so much that some couples chose to live together outside marriage, but when children were involved, they needed a mother and a father who were committed to one another. I tried to avoid advising my daughter on how to live her life, but couldn't understand why she wasn't able to see that her way was not working. Jenny needed the stability of a father figure, one who would be around for the duration, and I was glad now to have an opportunity to provide that stability, at least for a little while. Of course, this arrangement would probably be short-lived. Based on past experience, I imagined Patty would soon find someone new and wouldn't be staying here for long. I would just have to do the best I could, taking things one day at a time.

Stopping by the kitchen, I took a Coors Lite from the refrigerator. Then I returned to my computer, sat in my high-backed leather chair—one of my few extravagances—and sipped the beer, trying once more to think of something meaningful to write. I couldn't concentrate, though, and kept looking out the window toward the old lady's house, now masked completely by the thick fog. Should I go over there and see about her? I again wondered.

Probably I should, although that was the last place I wanted to be. Besides, all those dogs might eat me alive before I could proceed through the yard and get to the old lady's door. Still, what if she needed help? I couldn't just sit here and ignore her request—if one could call her strange ramblings a request. I just couldn't seem to shake the feeling that something was wrong.

After thinking about it for a few more minutes, I finished my beer in one gulp, got up, took my coat off the coat rack, put it on and reached for the doorknob.

Chapter 4

Patty's decision was suddenly made for her as her minivan sideswiped the steel guardrail mounted a few feet to the right of the highway. Careening back into the road, she found herself directly in the path of the oncoming vehicle. The half-ton Chevrolet pickup struck the Caravan a glancing blow just behind the passenger side door, causing the van to spin sharply. Patty's head banged into the driver's side window, nearly knocking her unconscious. Then from the corner of her eye, she watched in horror as the collision threw Jenny against the dash, then hard against the door.

The van suddenly rolled onto its top. Sounds of scraping metal and breaking glass drowned out Patty's screams. She grabbed for her little girl, who continued to tumble first one way and then another.

The visual scene then switched to slow motion in her mind as Patty, unable to reach Jenny, could only watch helplessly as her little girl somersaulted back and forth across the rolling vehicle. Barbie dolls flew in all directions, as did other items from various locations in the van. A suitcase slammed against the backseat, scattering clothes throughout. Everything not fastened down catapulted through the air, bouncing off windows, doors, seats, the overhead and floor. A McDonalds bag exploded against the driver's side window, its contents spilling all over Patty's head.

Suddenly the passenger side door flew open. Patty screamed in horror as she watched her little girl pitch out onto the pavement.

"NO! Oh, God! NO! NO! This can't be happening. . .it's just a dream.

Patty continued to scream as her car rolled, bounced and slid, finally coming to rest upside-down near the guardrail. In the background, Patty heard a hissing sound. She saw steam or smoke pouring into the van. The smell of gasoline made her nauseous. Her head felt as if it would explode.

Vaguely, she noticed the radio was still playing. Maria was just finishing the song: ". . . I simply remember my favorite things. . .and then I don't feel so bad."

Oh, God, please. . .please let Jenny be all right. Let this all be just a nightmare!

Realizing she had to get to her daughter, Patty looked out through the window into the fog and smoke. She couldn't see Jenny anywhere. Frantically, she clawed at the seatbelt harness, which held her suspended upside-down, already making breathing difficult.

Then through the fog she suddenly glimpsed the lifeless body of her little girl, lying across the highway—so still.

NO! This can't be real. It's just a dream, that's all this is. I'll wake up soon. Oh, God, please. . .please let her be all right.

As Patty struggled to grasp the seatbelt release, her fingers suddenly touched something soft and sticky. Moving her hand in front of her face, she noticed a dark red substance clinging to her fingers.

Oh, God. . .NO! Blood!

But no...not blood. She almost laughed aloud. She had stuck her hand into the red icing from Jenny's birthday cake that Patty had bought right before leaving. Tomorrow was Jenny's birthday. She was going to be eight years old.

IS! She IS going to be eight years old! Oh, God! What have I done to my baby?

Glancing around at the disarray inside the van, Patty noticed red velvet cake scattered and smeared all around the interior.

Please, God! Let her be all right.

Without thinking, Patty licked her fingers and found that the icing tasted good. Then again facing reality, she screamed, "Help! Somebody, help!"

But no one seemed to hear her.

Please God. . .help me. . .please. . .

Time stood still as she hung there, upside-down in her car seat. She tried to make her mind work. Couldn't think clearly. Pain shot through her head from front to back, then caromed from side to side. Nausea suddenly swept through her body. She felt dizzy, lightheaded. She fought to remain conscious.

Somehow, she had to get the damned seatbelt unfastened. But the more she fumbled with the release, the more frustrated she became. Exasperated, she gave a final jerk on the buckle and somehow, the belt popped loose. Patty fell hard against the top of the upside-down vehicle, her head striking the roof with a thud. For an instant, she saw stars and fought to remain conscious.

Shaking her head to clear it, Patty sat up. She tried to open the door, first pushing the handle in the wrong direction because it was upside-down. She pushed, pulled and jerked, but now that she was free of the seat belt, the damned door wouldn't budge. No matter how hard she yanked at the handle, it would not open. She began banging her fists against the window and continued until her knuckles were raw and bruised. Still, she remained trapped. She screamed until her throat hurt, and then she began to cry. Bitter bile poured into her throat as she fought to keep from vomiting.

Please, God, please. . .somebody help me!

Finally, through the fog she glimpsed a shadow. Her breath caught in her throat. Someone was approaching—perhaps the driver of the other vehicle, her muddled mind reasoned. Suddenly a man jerked open her car door and Patty tumbled out onto the asphalt. Quickly jumping up, she stumbled blindly across the road toward Jenny, who still lay motionless on the damp, black pavement.

"I've killed her! I've killed her. Oh, God! I've killed my little girl!" Patty screamed as she fell onto her knees beside the lifeless little girl.

By now, two other cars had stopped and a few people had begun to gather around. Someone must already have called 911, because Patty thought she heard the sound of approaching sirens—*sireens*, as Jenny called them. Patty reached down and lifted her little girl's head. She wanted to pick her up, to hold her in her arms, yet she was afraid to move her. Jenny might have broken bones and moving her could make things worse. *Oh God! How could they be worse!* Jenny appeared unconscious and

Patty noticed a trickle of blood on her forehead. Her tiny body felt so lifeless, like a rag doll.

Feeling her world spinning out of control, Patty continued to fight to remain conscious. She swallowed repeatedly, trying to force back the sour contents of her stomach that kept rising into her throat. Chills swept through her body as she sat there, just holding her little girl.

Patty sat there in a dream-like state for what could have been hours, but was most likely only a few minutes. She rocked back and forth, holding Jenny's head in her lap. After what seemed an awfully long time, an ambulance finally arrived. Some men rushed over with a stretcher. Carefully, they took the little girl from Patty. In a daze, she watched them place her little girl on the stretcher and carry her away. Next, they lifted Patty onto a stretcher and rushed her toward a waiting ambulance. As they placed her inside, everything in her world went black.

Patty awoke sometime later to strangely unfamiliar surroundings. It sounded as if she was in a hospital emergency room. Seeing a nurse standing beside her, Patty screamed, "Jenny! Where's my baby? Is she all right?"

"Now just relax, ma'am," the nurse said in a practiced, calm voice. She smiled perfunctorily and touched Patty on the shoulder. "The doctors are helping your little girl. I'm sure everything will be all right."

Patty tried to sit up. "Is she conscious? Can I see her?"

"I'm uh. . .I'm not sure. Now please, lie down and just try to relax. Please lie still. I have to check your blood pressure and pulse."

Everything will be all right! Oh, God! That's what they always say, particularly when it isn't true! Ignoring the nurse's instructions, Patty again tried to sit up. As she rose toward a sitting position, a seething pain exploded inside her head and the room began to spin violently. She fell back onto the gurney, nausea sweeping through her. Vaguely, she heard the nurse explaining something about a possible concussion and that Patty must remain stationary.

Some time later, another nurse arrived and said that Jenny was conscious, but that they were taking her to X-ray to try and determine why she couldn't seem to move her legs.

"Noooo!" screamed Patty. "Is it—is it her back?"

"They're not sure yet," the nurse replied.

As a young girl, Patty had fallen out of a tree and broken her back, but she had been lucky and her injury healed without serious problems. She knew, however, that such an injury could cause one to be paralyzed—perhaps forever, she realized, remembering Christopher Reeve. She would rather die than for Jenny to be paralyzed. There was no way she was ever going to forgive herself for causing this. No way!

Sometime later someone asked if there was anyone Patty wanted them to notify. Surprised that she hadn't thought of it earlier, she gave them her father's phone number.

Daddy, please hurry. I need you.

A young doctor entered and walked over to her. "Your daughter's back from X-ray," he began. "It appears she's had some trauma to her spine, but there doesn't seem to be any fracture. We've paged the on-call neurologist. He should be here soon."

In shock, Patty glared at the doctor. "What! What are you saying? What do you mean, *trauma* to her spine? Can she move her legs?"

The doctor averted his eyes. "Well, I'm afraid that's still a problem. But don't worry, the neurologist should be able to give us a better evaluation soon."

"Oh, God! What have I done to my baby? What have I done?"

Patty drifted into a stupor, real and imaginary events becoming nearly indistinguishable. Sounds from within the emergency room blended with her recollection of the cacophony from the accident scene. Everything crescendoed into the awful reality that she had caused her beautiful daughter to be critically injured. Mixed with this realization was her continued appeal to some higher power that this would all be just a dream—that she would awaken soon to find everything exactly as it should be. Reality, however, kept creeping back into her consciousness. She had caused Jenny to be paralyzed. There was no way she could ever live with herself.

Chapter 5

As I started out the door to head over toward the old lady's house, the phone on my desk rang. I froze, my hand on the doorknob. Then with a strange, sinking sensation in the pit of my stomach, I took a step back toward the desk. Something was wrong—I felt it, as I picked up the receiver during the middle of the third ring. Cringing, my heart sank as I listened in disbelief to the voice on the phone. As I replaced the receiver, I thought again of the old woman. Glancing through the fog toward the Wilson place, I saw her standing in the edge of the yard—motionless, like a statue. How could she possibly have known? I continued to stare in a daze as surreal image fade into the fog?

Even with a brief stop at the accident scene on the way down the mountain, I arrived at the hospital in Asheville forty minutes after receiving the fateful phone call. I had felt weak all over when I came upon the accident site, which was only about a mile from my house. I was shocked at the extent of the damage to the car as I saw them towing it away. The top and the rear end of the passenger side were crushed nearly beyond recognition. I stopped and explained who I was to the state trooper who seemed to be in charge of securing the site. I asked about Patty's and Jenny's condition, but the trooper could not—or more likely chose not to—tell him anything, other than that the accident victims had been rushed to the hospital. I asked how the accident had happened and then inquired about the condition of the driver of the other vehicle. The trooper told me that the other driver was an elderly man who lived on the other side of the mountain, and that he didn't seem to be seriously injured. The man had told the police that he'd had trouble seeing the centerline in the fog and wasn't aware he was on the wrong side of the road until too late to avoid colliding with the other vehicle.

A few minutes later, when I reached the freeway, I was glad to find there was hardly any traffic. Although a layer of fog still hung low in the valley, significantly reducing visibility, I set the cruise control to 90, and didn't slow until I approached the exit into downtown Asheville.

After pulling the Ford Explorer into a temporary parking space near the Emergency Room entrance, I rushed into the crowded lobby area. Typical of most ER's, this one was filled with people in various stages of discomfort, awaiting their turn at the admission desk. I understood that hospital emergency rooms were not what they once were, when most patients who came there were suffering from true emergencies. Nowadays, many people came to emergency rooms requesting treatment for various ailments that by no means qualified as emergencies. Since emergency rooms were not permitted to turn anyone away and were required to treat whomever showed up—regardless if they had insurance or were able to pay—most hospital ER's were continually packed with people awaiting their turn.

Squeezing my way through the crowd until I reached the counter, I interrupted a harried nurse, who seemed to be trying without much success to provide some order to the chaos.

"Carter—Patty Carter. I'm her father. And her little girl, Jenny. Are they here?"

While continuing to shuffle through some papers, she calmly replied, "Yes, sir, they're here. Just a minute and I'll have someone take you to them."

A few moments later, another nurse appeared and led me through the center of the ER and into a curtained-off cubicle in the rear, away from the main bustle. Patty was lying on a gurney, a team of two nurses and a young doctor administering to a wound on her head. Tom rushed to her side and took her hand.

"Hi, sweetheart. How ya doing?"

She looked up and tears filled her eyes. "Daddy! Dad, I'm so glad to see you. I'm okay. . .I think. It— it's Jenny. They said she—she can't move her legs, Daddy. It's all my fault. I should've waited, like you said. I'll never forgive myself."

I squeezed her hand as she sobbed. "They. . .they won't let me. . .see her. Please. . .make them let me see. . .my little girl."

I didn't know what to say or do. The young doctor turned and looked at me, smiled faintly and said, "She's being treated by the finest doctors, sir. I'm sure she'll be fine. You'll be able to see her soon."

"Thank you, Doctor. Can you tell us anything about her injuries?"

"Just what we've already told your daughter. The little girl has several cuts and bruises—nothing serious—and she suffered a mild concussion. She's had some possible trauma to her spinal cord, near lumbar vertebra one and two. But she doesn't appear to have any broken bones—and no compression fracture of her vertebra, which is not uncommon in these cases. She has a nasty lump on her head, but it doesn't appear too serious. The primary problem is that she can't seem to move her legs. That's what they're trying to diagnose now. We suspect it is temporary."

"I see, thank you," I replied, unable to think of anything else to ask.

Turning back to Patty, the doctor said, "We're going to admit you, ma'am, just so we can observe you overnight—just as a precaution."

When the doctor and nurses finished administering to Patty, they left and I continued to hold my daughter's hand. "This wasn't your fault, Patty. I talked to the trooper at the accident scene and he said the man coming down the mountain was on the wrong side of the road. There was nothing you could've done to prevent the accident."

"Except that I could've waited until later to come. . .like you told me I should. Was the. . .was the other driver hurt?"

"No, not bad, I don't think."

"Oh, Daddy, what are we going to do? I should never have tried to drive in. . .I've hurt my baby . . ."

"Patty, we can second-guess what we should've done to prevent any accident. You can't blame yourself for this. I'm sure Jenny will be fine. We'll just have to wait and see what the doctors determine."

They admitted Patty into a room on the fourth floor and I sat with her while awaiting news of Jenny. We questioned every nurse who came by, but none could—or would—tell us anything about what was going on. Patty kept mumbling about how the accident had been all her fault, and I continued trying to make her understand that she mustn't blame herself.

About an hour later, a middle-aged, gray-haired doctor entered the room. Exuding confidence, he smiled as he calmly walked over to us. "Hi, folks. Sorry to keep you waiting so long. I'm Doctor Greenfield, head of neurology. I've been looking into Jenny's injuries." He looked at Patty, his demeanor calm but serious. "Your daughter has suffered a mild concussion. She's conscious now and we don't believe this is going to cause any major problems. But we like to observe an injury like this for at least twenty-four hours, just to make sure."

The doctor then cleared his throat and glanced back and forth between us. "I'm afraid the more serious problem is the trauma to Jenny's spinal cord. We've taken X-rays and an MRI, and the good news is that she doesn't appear to have any broken bones. She's received some trauma, though, near the first and second lumbar region. We've scheduled a CAT scan."

Patty began sobbing. Her own back injury had been to her L1 vertebra, so she had some idea of the nature of this type injury.

"The fact that she cannot move her legs is not all that uncommon in these type cases," the doctor continued. "I'm confident she'll recover just fine. These type injuries usually require some physical therapy, though, and sometimes it can take several days—perhaps even weeks—to fully recover. We can't be sure how long in any individual case. Unfortunately, other than therapy and allowing time for healing, there's not much more we can do but watch and make sure there's no undue swelling or fluid accumulation around the traumatized area. Do either of you have any questions?"

"Yes, Doctor," Patty began. "When will she—I mean, how long will she have to stay in the hospital?"

The doctor shook his head. "I'm afraid I can only give you a best guess right now. If nothing further develops and we don't see anything unexpected when we get back the results of some other tests we've ordered, I would say she can probably go home in a couple of days. But don't hold me to that. She'll have to come back two or three times a week for therapy, though, and for us to check her progress. . .and that could continue for. . .well, we just don't know how long. Is that going to be a problem for you?"

Patty looked at me. "No problem, Doctor," I responded. "I only live about twenty miles away. They were on their way to visit me and they'll be staying for a while, so we can bring her back whenever necessary." I glanced at Patty and smiled. "They'll be staying with me at least until Jenny is well." I then took Patty's hand, squeezed it and she smiled weakly, tears forming in her eyes.

"Very well," the doctor concluded. "Feel free to call me if you think of any other questions. I'll get back to you if we find out anything more, and I'll be in to see you again in the morning in any case."

As the doctor started to walk out of the room, Patty called after him. "Doctor, can I. . .can I see her?"

Doctor Greenfield turned, smiled faintly and said, "Sure, I don't see any problem with your seeing her for a few minutes. We're admitting her into intensive care right now, where she'll remain overnight. When she's settled, I'll have one of the nurses there inform your nursing station and someone can take you up for a few minutes. She'll be sedated and will probably be sleeping, but you can see her for a few minutes." He smiled again, turned and walked out.

About an hour later, a nurse came in and notified us that Jenny was now settled in the ICU. The nurse then helped Patty into a wheelchair and took us to the unit, where we were allowed to go right in.

Jenny looked so tiny and helpless lying there in the bed, an IV in her right arm and wires running from various areas of her small body to machines that monitored her heart rate and other vitals. The nurse explained that Jenny was sleeping, that her vitals signs were all normal and that she would probably be moved to a private room tomorrow, assuming all went well throughout the night.

We stood in silence for a few minutes, staring down at the helpless looking little girl and listening to the whirring of the various machines designed to keep critically injured patients alive. I noticed tears in Patty's eyes and discreetly wiped away a tear of my own. Neither of us spoke, and after a few minutes we left and returned to Patty's room.

"She looked so. . .so tiny, Dad—so helpless," Patty said when we were back in her room. She then buried her face in her hands and began sobbing. "What have I. . .what have I done?"

Taking my daughter's hand, I said, "She'll be fine, I'm sure of it. Try not to blame yourself. This wasn't your fault." I didn't know what else to say.

I stayed with Patty throughout the night, sleeping fitfully in the plastic-covered, straight-backed chair next to her bed. Several times during my near sleepless night, I got up and went back to the ICU to confirm with the nurse there that Jenny was resting comfortably. Each time when I returned, I found Patty awake, demanding to know Jenny's condition.

Shortly after eight o'clock the next morning, Doctor Greenfield strode into Patty's room. "Good morning, folks. I've just been to see Jenny," he began cheerfully. "She's awake now and seems to be in pretty good spirits, considering." Clearing his throat, he continued, "She still cannot seem to move her legs, but of course, that's not...uh...unexpected. We're going to move her into a regular room later this morning so we can observe her for at least another twenty-four hours. If everything looks okay, we may release her tomorrow. We're going to discharge you this morning, Ms. Carter. You can go see your daughter as soon as she's moved into a room. That should be within the hour."

Patty smiled weakly. "Thank you, Doctor."

Two hours later, we stood in Jenny's room looking down at the little girl, who appeared much better than we had expected she might. She had a small bandage just above her right eye and another on the elbow of her right arm. There were also a few minor cuts and scrapes on her face and arms.

Jenny opened her eyes and smiled when she recognized us. "Hi, Ole Pa! Hi, Mommy! When can I go home?"

"Soon, sweetheart," Patty said, trying to smile. "The doctor says you can probably go home tomorrow. Happy birthday, sweetie. I'm so sorry that you. . .that you have to be . . ." Patty fought back her tears. "I'm sorry you have to be here for your. . .for your birthday. As soon as you're home, I'll make you a nice new birthday cake, I promise."

"It's okay, Mommy. Did you know I can't move my legs? Am I going to get a wheelchair for my birthday?"

I was amazed at how quickly children usually get right to the heart of an issue. Patty looked at me and bit her lower lip, unsuccessfully attempting to force back her tears.

"Jenny, the doctors think you're going to be fine," I began. "It'll just take some time. You'll probably be in a wheelchair for a few days, and we'll be coming back here every couple of days for some therapy sessions. The doctors think you're going to recover with no problems. It'll just take some time."

"Oh, okay," Jenny said, then screwed up her face into a puzzled look. "What's *therapy*, Ole Pa?"

I chuckled. "Oh, just some exercises to help you to be able to use your legs again, that's all. It won't hurt, I promise. It'll probably be lots of fun."

"Okay, Ole Pa." Jenny then looked at her mother. "Mommy, how come ya got a bandage on your head? Are you okay?"

"Yes, sweetie, I'm fine. Just got a bump on my head. . .sort of like yours."

"Mine doesn't hurt much, does yours?"

"No, not much."

"Mommy, are my Barbies okay?"

"Oh, uh...I'm sure they're... all right. We'll check later, okay? How about a new Barbie for your birthday? Would you like that?"

"Oh, yes! Can I have Princess Barbie? Pleeease, Mommy. I've been wanting her for a long time."

"Yes, of course you can, sweetie. If we can find her around here, that is." Patty looked at me and added, "I bet Ole Pa would be happy to go and look for her."

"Okay, Mommy."

Jenny blinked several times and her eyelids began to droop. "I'm sleepy, Mommy," she mumbled softly. "Is it okay if I go to sleep now?"

"Yes, of course. Ole Pa and I will be right here when you wake up. Hopefully by tomorrow you'll be able to go home, okay?"

Jenny yawned and rubbed her eyes. "Okay, Mommy."

We stood watching until Jenny appeared to be sound asleep, then we walked silently out of her room and down the hallway to Patty's room, neither of us speaking of what was on both our minds.

Chapter 6

The old woman turned over in bed and squinted at the clock on her bedside table: 5:15 a.m., almost time to get up and perform her morning routine with her babies. She had to feed all her cats and dogs, and she had to let out the dogs that were inside and bring in some of the others.

Let's see... today it'll be Krissie, the Collie, and Randy, the horny little Terrier and. . .is it Sugar's turn today? No, she was inside yesterday. Then she remembered. It was the big black Lab, the one she had recently acquired, the one she called Omega. Now where had that name come from? And what did it mean, anyway? Vaguely, from somewhere in the recesses of her mind, she seemed to recall that Omega meant *last,* and this disturbed her. Of course, bringing him inside would require moving Jessica and Myrtie, her two big Persian cats, into the other room. For some reason, Omega didn't seem to like those two, although he never bothered her other cats. Oh well, he would just have to get used to them.

Clara Wilson had to get up and get this done soon. She couldn't allow the neighbors to see the same group of dogs in her yard on two consecutive days. Those nosy people next door—not Carter, of course, he was nice, although he had also complained once about her dogs waking him, when she had gone over to apologize for their bothering him. He hadn't been the one to call the health department on her, though—at least, she didn't think so—no doubt, it was those people who lived on the other side. What were their names? Peterson, or something like that—Jack and Jill, Clara called them. That stupid bitch Jill had stopped in front of her house just last week and warned Clara again that she had to do something about those barking dogs. She'd wanted to tell the bitch to go to hell, but she hadn't said anything.

Why couldn't they just mind their own damned business and leave her the hell alone? This was her property and she could do whatever she bloody well pleased on her own property, couldn't she? If she wanted to have a few dogs and cats—well, okay, maybe more than a few—it was none of their damned business. Didn't they understand that these were her babies. Well, at least the dogs kept people from coming into her yard. Too bad about that salesman who had tried to come to her door last week, though. Fortunately, Clara had come out when she heard the commotion, and the man had only gotten a few bites on his legs. Well, he should have paid more attention to the sign and stayed out of her yard.

Mercy, I've got to stop using such foul language. If Jake heard me, he'd get mad and scold me. Of course, he probably wouldn't hear her now, since he'd been dead for nearly five years. And she wasn't actually speaking out loud, anyway—was she? Suddenly, she wondered if they had buried Jake deeply enough. Sometime soon she had to check and make sure.

Clara never cursed when speaking with other people, only when talking to herself. Of course, she didn't usually speak much with others anyway. They all considered her insane, when they were the ones who were crazy. Oh, the nicer ones called her things like *eccentric* or *senile*, but they all meant the same thing. If only they knew what she had to go through every day—especially at night—then maybe they would be more understanding. She wondered how those people would feel if they were never allowed to sleep, or if they could foresee things coming before they happened, yet still not be able to do anything to stop them.

Clara didn't know why she used such language when talking to herself now. She hadn't always talked this way. She couldn't even remember when she had begun cursing so much. For some reason, it made her feel good, though—except when she worried about whether or not it was a sin and she was going to hell. Probably it was a sin—but no matter, she was fairly certain where she would be going, anyway. Too bad she couldn't ask Jake about that; he would know, of course. Strangely, she hadn't seen him around lately. During the first year or so after he died, she had seen him frequently. Sometimes he would wander around the house late at night, although he never talked to her then. She wondered if perhaps they had sent him to that awful place down below by now. Maybe that was why he never came around anymore. Probably that was where they would have sent him. After all, he had violated at least five of the Ten Commandments, and some more than once, too. Maybe he had violated even more, but she only knew about the five. Screwing her sister, Pauline, that had been one of his worst violations—surely that counted for at least two violations—and then, of course, lying about it for all those years afterwards. Clara had known about that all along, though, so he hadn't needed to lie. She knew about his other women, too, but what he did with Pauline had been the worst. Clara should have killed him for that—and Pauline, too. She hadn't done it, though—at least she didn't think she had. Still, they were both dead now, so perhaps . . .

Well, maybe she would see Jake again down *there* before too much longer, since probably that was where they planned to send her too. Every day, and especially at night when she was afraid to go to sleep, Clara expected to see herself dying. Nothing had come to her yet in that regard, though, so maybe it wasn't quite time for her to go. She would know, of course, because she always knew these kinds of things. She would see them in her mind shortly before they happened for real. She had known before Jake died and had tried to tell him so that he could prepare; but of course, he wouldn't listen. He never listened to anything she had to say. Anyway, it would have been too late by then.

A tear stole down the old lady's cheek as she remembered that Gordy, her big German Shepherd—her favorite—would be leaving her in a couple of days. Last night while walking, Clara, in her mind, had seen him die. He had just laid down on the porch, closed his eyes and suddenly he was gone. Thankfully, he wouldn't have to suffer. Of course, he was old, like her, so perhaps it was his time. *Let's see, to figure the dog's age in human years, you multiply the dog's age by seven. . .so seven times eleven—or is it twelve? Oh well, if I multiply by eleven-and-a-half that would be about, let's see. . .about eighty-two or eighty-three. Hmmm. . .yes, old Gordy's just about my age, all right, give or take a year or two.*

Maybe that was how she would go too; just lie down, close her eyes and never wake up. Naturally, that was why Clara seldom allowed her eyes to close. She was afraid she might never open them again. She had learned long ago to sleep without fully closing her eyes, which of course was why she walked so much, especially at night. Didn't they understand that if she stayed in bed all night, she might close her eyes and go to sleep? If that happened, she would probably never wake up, so she usually only allowed herself to sleep while walking. At first, she had run into some trees and a fence or two, but that didn't happen often anymore. She at first worried that she might walk right off the bluff, though, so she had learned to stay far enough away from the brow to prevent that from happening.

It hadn't always been this way, of course. Before, when Jake was working at that job in the city, when their little girl was growing up, Clara had been happy. Or had she? She had once thought so, but now she wasn't so sure if she had ever been happy. She had felt happier then, though, especially before her eyes had begun failing her. It bothered her that she couldn't see well enough to drive at night anymore. Sometimes she worried about what she would do if something happened requiring her to have to go down the mountain after dark. She wouldn't ask anyone for help, of course, no matter what. Probably Carter next door would help her, if she asked him, but she would never ask; she didn't want to be beholden to anyone.

Her no-good slut of a daughter could help, too—if she would. Clara hadn't spoken to that hussy for years, though, not since she left the last time with that awful man, after saying all those horrible things about never wanting to see her mother again. Deep down, Clara was aware that she had driven her daughter away; but still, the bitch could at least call or come by occasionally. She had come to her father's funeral, but she hadn't spoken to her mother then and had left immediately after the service. Clara hadn't seen or heard from her since, and didn't care now if she ever saw her again.

The things Clara saw in her mind were what bothered her the most now—things she foresaw before they happened—or as they were happening, such as with that poor little girl. She was sorry about that, and especially dreaded what Carter was about to have to endure. He seemed like such a nice man. He had given her that nice new flashlight for her birthday. She still wondered how he had known it was her birthday.

In her mind, Clara had seen the little girl again last night. A pretty young woman, probably the little girl's mother, was pushing her up the sidewalk in a wheelchair over at Carter's house. So, the girl would be coming there soon, and she would be staying for a long time. She wouldn't be running around outside playing, though, because she would have to stay in that wheelchair all the time. This made Clara sad and she tried to think of some way she might help. Maybe the little girl liked kittens or puppies. Most little girls did. Clara might let her play with one of the puppies or one of her cats. Maybe she would even give her one of the kittens that had been born a few weeks ago.

What was that little girl's name, anyway? Maybe it was Jenny, the name she had called her own little girl. Such a nice name, Jenny. That's what she would call the little girl, Clara decided. Jenny was coming home soon and maybe it would be just like old times. The more she thought about it, the more excited she became. Before long, Clara convinced herself that this might be *her* Jenny, coming back after all these years. That didn't seem possible, of course, but Clara had learned by now that nearly anything was possible—anything she could create in her mind, that is.

The old woman looked at the clock again and realized she had to hurry; soon it would be daylight. She sat up on the edge of her bed and put her bare feet on the cold tile floor. With her arthritic, knobby fingers, she pulled her bathrobe around her naked body. She had to remain nude while in bed, of course, and sometimes she got cold, especially when he didn't come. Still, she had to be ready for him in case he did come.

The worst part was when she saw herself naked in the mirror nowadays. Clara hated what had happened to her body, the parts all drooping and sagging. Her once resilient breasts now hung nearly to her waist, or to where her waist had once been. They looked like deflated balloons that had been blown up a few too many times, stretching them into long, wrinkled pouch-like shapes. The skin around her protruding stomach hung in wrinkled folds, and the flab on her skinny arms reminded her of an old washboard. Her legs didn't look quite as bad, probably because of all the walking, she imagined.

Fortunately, *he* didn't seem to mind how she looked, as long as she was ready for him when he climbed into her bed at night. He hadn't come for a long time now, though, so perhaps he was never coming again.

Gordy's going to die tomorrow, she again remembered, and tears filled her eyes. Gordy had always been her favorite. Well, maybe she would invite her new baby into her bed soon. *Now, what is his name? Oh, yes, Omega*—the last. *Maybe Omega will keep me warm now. Of course, he'll first have to learn to get along with the cats.*

After finishing her morning chores, Clara sat in her rocking chair in front of the window facing Carter's driveway, waiting and watching for the little girl to arrive. She knew Jenny would be coming sometime today, although she didn't know exactly when it would be.

Just before noon, the old woman saw Carter's blue Ford Explorer turn into the driveway. Her heart raced as she watched Carter and a young blond woman help the pretty little girl out of the car. She continued to watch as Carter carried a child-sized wheelchair into the house. Clara picked up two of her favorite cats, went outside and began walking up and down the road between her house Carter's house, hoping she might get a chance to see the little girl closer up.

After a few minutes, Clara became tired, so she returned home. Probably they would keep the little girl inside all day today anyway. Besides, Clara still had to figure out some way to make Jenny like her again. She tried to remember what she had done to cause her Jenny to turn against her, but she couldn't think of anything specific.

Throughout the day and into the night, Clara remained troubled. She just couldn't figure out how Jenny had gotten so small again, or why her little girl was staying over there at Carter's house now, when she should be here with her mother. Clara realized, of course, that this couldn't be her Jenny; after all, her Jenny didn't even exist anymore. Still, in the back of her mind, she allowed for the possibility that this little girl might be her Jenny, come back after all these years to give her another chance. This time she would do it right.

Chapter 7

The morning was unusually warm and sunny for an early spring day. I referred to these kinds of days as *California days*. Having spent a great portion of my naval career in San Diego, California, I had learned to take these kinds of days for granted, since the weather there was bright and sunny a majority of the time, with temperatures usually ranging from the low seventies to low eighties, and a cool ocean breeze prevailing most of the time. Now, whenever a day like this one came along, I tried to remember to appreciate it.

As I backed my Explorer out of the garage and proceeded slowly down the driveway, I waved to Jenny, who was sitting out on the front porch enjoying the sunshine and playing with her new Princess Barbie that I had bought her. My mission this morning was to locate Patty's car, ascertain the extent of the damage and determine whether it was fixable. Patty was going to call the insurance company this morning to report the accident and find out what they were going to do. Another important task that I had to perform was to retrieve Patty's luggage from her car so she and Jenny would have clean clothes. I had also promised Jenny that I would try to find her Barbie dolls. I dreaded the tasks ahead of me, but considered this a duty that only I could perform. Patty should never have to experience the trauma of seeing that car again.

My tenseness increase as I rounded the curve through the cut in the bluff and approached the accident site. First, I noticed the skid marks on the asphalt and other markings where the blue paint and metal from Patty's van had scraped the pavement. I cringed as I looked at the guardrail running alongside the bluff. This piece of bent metal had prevented the van from plunging over a straight drop-off of about a hundred feet. One section of the railing was streaked with blue paint that had scraped off the Caravan when it sideswiped the guardrail, propelling the car back into the path of the oncoming truck. But as bad as the collision had been, it would have been deadly had the van plunged over the cliff.

As I got closer, something on the side of the road caught my eye. A bright colored object lay on the shoulder of the road, near the place where Patty's car had turned over. I slowed down, pulled over to the side of the road, got out and walked across the highway toward the object. With a lump in my throat, I picked up a tiny Barbie doll and turned it over in my hands, glad to see that it didn't appear to be hurt badly. The doll's clothes were a little dirty, but otherwise the blond-haired beauty appeared intact. Looking around the area for a few moments, I saw nothing else of interest, so I got back into the Explorer and continued down the mountain.

As I was parking in front of Hawkins' body shop, I noticed the blue Caravan—or what was left of it— nestled among several other wrecked vehicles near the front of the shop. I vaguely remembered this garage from when I was growing up here, but

Hawkins hadn't owned the business way back then. I seemed to remember that someone named Inman had once owned this garage, but I could be mistaken. Of course, it didn't matter anyway. It seemed the business had grown over the years. Numerous wrecked vehicles, most in need of major bodywork— or more likely in need of a tow to the junkyard— cluttered the whole area around the building.

I got out and walked inside. The noise was nearly deafening as men with hammers, grinders and various other pneumatic tools labored to restore the sheet-metal bodies of wrecked vehicles on which they labored. The place reeked from a mixture of oil, grease, paint and residue from countless body parts that had been sanded down to bare metal, the dust of their old paint filling the air and settling on everything in sight. I wondered how anyone could tolerate working in this type environment. The noise and smell alone were enough to make me anxious to conduct my business and quickly depart.

No one paid me any mind, so I went over to one of the men, and yelling above the noise, asked where I might find Mr. Hawkins. The man pointed to a small room off to the side of the main work area, so I headed in that direction.

The makeshift office turned out to be nearly as greasy and messy as the surrounding area. A large man sat behind a desk that seemed much too small for him, its surface covered with pieces of smudged paperwork. The man might have been near the same age as I, although it appeared the years had taken a greater toll on him. He was unshaven, his greasy hair was long and unkempt, and his blue chambray uniform—if it could be called a uniform—reeked of grease and grime. The clothes looked as if they hadn't been washed in weeks, much like the man wearing them. As I entered, the man looked up, his gruff expression revealing his unhappiness at being interrupted.

After a brief hostile stare, he spat a stream of tobacco juice toward a can beside his desk, missing, and mumbled, "Yeah?"

"Sorry to bother you; I'm looking for Mr. Hawkins?"

"Well, ya found 'im!" rumbled Hawkins in a surly voice. After chewing for a moment on the large wad of tobacco in his jaw, he turned his head sideways and added in a slightly less hostile tone, "What'd ya need?"

Quickly introducing myself, I told Hawkins why I was there. Hawkins struggled to his feet, kicked back his chair and grimaced, revealing two missing front teeth. He reached across the desk and offered me his grease-blackened hand. Involuntarily hesitating, I then grasped the extended hand gingerly.

Obviously more friendly now that he had determined I was likely a paying customer, Hawkins offered, "Come on outside." He squeezed past me and led me back outside into the work bay. I followed the big man through the grime and grease toward the front entrance. Noise from within the shop prevented conversation, as the men with their obnoxious sounding machinery seemed to be competing with one another to see who could add most to the cacophony.

Once outside, Hawkins walked directly to the Caravan. He spat a stream of tobacco juice onto the ground, then said, "Recken she's totaled. We could fix her up, all right, but it'd be costin' y'all more'n that van's worth. As y'n see, the whole right side and top would have to be replaced. And the door and two wheels. . .not to mention the damage underneath. Frame's prob'bly warped, too. Ain't no way hit'd ever drive rat again, even if'n we fixed it."

As we walked around the van surveying the damage, Hawkins turned his head to one side and spat another stream of brown tobacco juice onto the ground. I grimaced, agreeing that the van did not appear fixable. I only hoped for Patty's sake that the insurance adjuster would concur. It seemed miraculous that only the one window on the passenger-side sliding door had been shattered. I continued to wince as I examined the vehicle, imagining the trauma that Patty and Jenny must have endured. Having never been in an accident of anywhere near this magnitude, I thanked God no one had been more seriously injured.

Hawkins spat another stream of tobacco juice, then looked at me and nodded his head. "We could take yer money and fix 'er up, aw'ight—where hit'd look pert'near good as new. Wouldn't be right, though. Don't work that away. . . no sir-ee. Gonna tell ya how it is up front. Onliest way we'n stay in bidness is t' do rat by our cust'mers. Treat 'em fair and they'll keep acomin' back, ya see what I mean?"

"Yes, I agree. Well, thank you for being up front with me, Mr. Hawkins. I'd like to get some things out of the van now, if you don't mind—luggage and some other things."

"Shore, he'p yerse'f. I gotta git back to m' paperwork enyhow. Damned inshor'nce comp'nies keep on puttin' more'n more paperwork on us. Guess I'm gonna hafta har' me a girl to take keer of it all, or maybe git me one 'em *cum*-puters. Take alla time ya need, Carter."

"Thanks. I'll come in and let you know when I'm finished."

Hawkins headed back inside and I approached the vehicle cautiously, noting various items scattered around the interior: pieces of Barbie clothing, dried scraps of Jenny's birthday cake, clothes from a suitcase that had broken open, along with books, papers, crayons and paper bags bearing the McDonalds' insignia. The passenger side door was jammed in an open position and I couldn't help envisioning Jenny flying out through that door.

Forcing myself to climb into the van, I began searching through the debris, first gathering all the clothes I could find and putting them back into the suitcase. Next, I located two of Jenny's Barbie dolls and several pieces of Barbie clothing, which I placed into a paper bag that I found behind the front seat. Two other pieces of luggage were in the back storage compartment, seemingly intact, so I took them, along with the other items I had gathered, and put them into the Explorer. Then I made another quick pass through the cluttered interior of the Caravan, looking for anything of value that I might have missed. Seeing nothing else that I thought Patty and Jenny would need, I climbed out and took a few deep breaths in an effort to calm myself. Then I headed back into the body shop, making my way through the grease, grime and noise to thank Mr. Hawkins and let him know I was leaving.

"Like I tole ye, Carter," Hawkins said, glancing up from his paperwork, "we'n shore fix 'er up. . .but I wouldn't recommend it. Best bet is to total it an' git yerse'f a new'un. Ain't gonna never be happy with this here'un, nohow. I'n use some stuff off'n it fer parts, but it ain't gonna be worth more'n a couple hunnert dollars fer junk value. I been in this here bidness long 'nuff to know how it's gonna be. Y'n trust me, Carter. I ain't agonna steer ya wrong."

"Yes, I believe that, Mr. Hawkins, and I appreciate it. Well, we'll be in touch later about the disposition. If there's anything I didn't find, I may have to come back and look some more later...if that's all right."

"Come on by eny time y'all want. Hope yer gran'daughter gits okay soon. Heard she was hurt purty bad in the wreck."

"Thanks, I think she's going to be fine. Well, good day to you, Mr. Hawkins. And thanks again."

Hawkins spat tobacco juice toward the can beside his desk, adding to the accumulation on the floor around the can, then said, "Shore thang."

I drove slowly back through town and headed up the mountain. Seeing the condition of the Caravan had shaken me more than I had anticipated. Again, I thanked God that neither Patty nor Jenny had been hurt any worse than they had.

Of course, it was still possible that Jenny might never walk again, I reminded myself. Doctor Greenfield had assured us that her condition was temporary, though, and that she should be walking again soon. From observing the extent of damage to the van, I had also considered that it would probably take a long time for Patty and Jenny to recover from the trauma and possible damage to their psyche that must have occurred during the accident.

As I drove back up the mountain and again approached the accident site, I viewed it with a whole new perspective. After examining the van, I could now picture in my mind how the vehicle must have rolled and bounced to produce the damage I'd observed. I knew I would never again be able to pass this place without cringing. Apprehension about whether Jenny might ever walk again, along with how I was ever going to convince Patty that the accident and Jenny's injury had not been Patty's fault, continued to overpower all of my other emotions.

Chapter 8

The battered red 1989 Ford F-250 pickup wheeled sharply into the parking lot of the Red Dog Saloon, slid on some loose gravel, then came to a lurching halt beside a black F-150 pickup of about the same vintage. Nearly all the patrons of the Red Dog drove pickups of one sort or another. Most were full-sized Fords, Chevys or Dodge Rams, with gun racks mounted in the rear window, and with Confederate flags affixed in one place or another. Nearly all the trucks were American made, as hardly any of the type fellows who frequented the Red Dog Saloon would have ever considered driving one of those small foreign-made pickups, which they considered toys for sissies. Many of the trucks in the parking lot displayed bumper stickers proclaiming such things as *The South Will Rise Again*, *Yankee Go Home*, or something of that nature.

Occasionally, as was the case tonight, a car or two sat parked in front of the place. This usually indicated there were unattached females inside, although sometimes these vehicles belonged to some candy-assed city fellows who had decided they wanted to play *urban cowboy* for a night. These guys provided ready prey for the normal Red Dog patrons, who usually ended up kicking the city slickers' asses before the night was over. Maybe there would be a couple of them here tonight, Kirby Lawson considered. Kicking some behind was definitely a desirable item to include in his agenda for this evening. If there were women here, perhaps that would be just as well—hell, maybe even better. He would be happy to give them what they obviously came here for. In any case, he decided this was going to be a great evening...maybe just like the old days—before the bitch and her snotty-nosed kid had come into his life and curtailed most of his fun times.

A steady drizzle had been falling since around noon, accelerating the early evening twilight and adding bright, shimmering tinges to the normally muted Red Dog neon sign mounted above the entrance to the bar. The steady downpour chilled Kirby to the bone, matching his insidious, downtrodden mood that had slowly been spreading throughout every fiber of his being during the few days since *she* had taken off. In addition to dampening his spirits, the rain also ensured that even the small amount of aluminum siding business that might otherwise have come Kirby's way in this off season had to be put on hold. Of course, with the woman splitting on him unexpectedly like that, he was in no mood or position to conduct much business now anyway. At least she could have given him a little notice or a chance to explain.

No doubt the little girl had babbled some lies to her mother about what he had done to her. Hell, he hadn't done anything to her; certainly, he hadn't hurt her. Actually, he had tried to be nice to her, simply wanting to tuck her in and tell her goodnight, since her mother was out having a good time, leaving him to baby-sit the kid. The little girl had already mastered some of her mother's teasing gestures. Women were all the same, no matter their age, every one of them out to make a man crazy in one way or another. Even at the age of seven or eight, some already had those techniques practically mastered. Truth be known, most of them were probably born with it.

Kirby had once been a steady patron of the Red Dog Saloon, although he hadn't been here often during the past few months. *She* always wanted him to stay home, and he had foolishly given in to her most of the time; otherwise, she wouldn't give him what he wanted. He still maintained contact with a couple of his drinking buddies from days past, though, and was happy now to see Jack Larkin's big Dodge Ram pickup in the parking lot. Kirby and Jack had been high school classmates, and over the years they had worked together on several construction jobs, before Kirby had started his own business. They had also done their share of drinking, brawling and womanizing. Kirby hoped they might perform at least two—if not all three—of these activities before this night was over. As he ambled inside, he told himself that he didn't much care in which order they came.

"Well, I'll be a damned! Look what the dogs done drug in," Jack Larkin said, punching his buddy on the shoulder. "Your old lady let you outta the cave for a night, huh?"

Kirby sat heavily on the barstool next to his buddy. He caught the bartender's eye—happy to see Suzie on duty tonight—and pointed to the long-necked Budweiser on the bar in front of Jack. Suzie smiled, winked and slid another down the bar to Kirby.

"Go to hell!" Kirby said, punching Jack on the shoulder, slightly harder than he might otherwise have. "You just wish you had one of 'em in your cave."

"Yeah, right! You know that's so. Specially if she looked like Patty-babe."

Kirby took a swig of his beer, then said, "That bitch done took off on me."

"What? She left you?"

"You catch on fast."

"Well, I'll be damned! What'd she do, catch ya screwing 'round on her?"

"Hell, I don't know. Typical broad, I guess. Ya know how they are. Can't never figure out why they do nothing they do."

"Yeah, I know what ya mean, Kirb."

Kirby glanced around the joint, recognizing a few of the regulars. He noticed a couple of women sitting in a booth over in the corner, although from where he sat, they didn't look like they would be worth much effort. Of course, the evening was young yet. As it wore on, they might become lots better looking. By midnight, they might even be looking like super models. It appeared that Buck Thompson and Bobby Joe, a couple of the regular *lounge lizards*, were already making a move on the women, though, so Kirby turned back to the bar and took a long swill of his Bud.

"I bet she caught ya messin' 'round on her," Jack said, winking at Kirby. "Ya didn't beat her up or nothin' like that, did ya?"

"Hell no! Probably should have, though. Sure as hell would now if I could find the bitch," Kirby said, downing the rest of his beer and motioning Suzie to bring him another.

"What'd she do, just up and leave ya for no good reason, without even tellin' ya where she was goin' or nothin'?"

"What I'd just say?"

"You mean ya ain't got no idea where she went?"

"Never said I ain't got *no* idea. Got me an idea, all right. Just don't know the address. She went running off to *daddy*, I expect—somewhere down in North Carolina. . .around Asheville, I think."

"One 'em *daddy's girls*, huh? Yeah, I know the type. Ya gonna go after her, or what?"

"Said I didn't know where she was, didn't I? Don't you ever listen?"

"I heard ya, peckerwood. How hard would it be to find her, though. . .if ya really wanted to?"

"Hell, I don't know. She never told me where the ole man moved to. I think it was to some little town in North Carolina, somewhere near where he growed up, I guess. Never did give much of a damn about it. I was just glad the bastard left—never did like the sum-bitch. She never woulda moved in with me if he hadn't gone."

"She didn't never talk about where he went? Never called him or nothin'?"

"Hell, I don't know. . .maybe. She went down there once for a couple days. Mighta mentioned where she was goin'. I didn't pay no attention." Kirby took another long swig of his Bud.

"Seems like she woulda called him sometimes."

"Yeah, I guess so. What the hell difference does it make, anyway?"

Kirby and Jack both gulped the last of their Buds and Suzie quickly brought them two more.

"Thought ya wanted to find her, Kirb."

"I dunno, Jack. I'd like to, that's for sure. It's been sorta eatin' away at me ever since she split. Know what I mean?"

"Hell yes! They always want ya to give 'em ever'thang they want, then when some little something don't go their way, they just up and split. Been there—done that. Most of 'em ain't worth chasin' after nohow, though...that's for sure. They all got the same equipment—if ya seen one ya seen 'em all."

"Ya got that right! Pisses me off, though, her just leaving like that without no good reason and no explanation. Kinda left me hanging in the lurch."

"How's that?"

"She's been doing all my paperwork and stuff, ya know, trying to help me get this business going. Now I ain't got no idea where nothin' is. Ya know how women are about organizing ever'thang just the way they want it. Now I can't find nothin'."

"I know what ya mean. So, ya gonna try to call 'er, or what?"

"Said I didn't know the phone number! How many times I gotta tell ya stuff?"

"Ain't ya got it on an old phone bill or something? Surely she musta called her old man sometime durin' all the time she lived with ya. The number'd be on the phone bills if she did, wouldn't it?"

"Hell, I dunno. . .I guess so. Hadn't never thought about it. Ain't much need'n calling her noway, though. I might just up'n go down there—if I knew where she was, that is. Ya know, just show up. Guess if I slapped her around a little I'd feel some better about it all, anyway."

"Might find the address on the Internet."

"Huh?"

"The Internet. Ain't ya never heard of the Internet?"

"Yeah, I heard of the damned Internet! So what?"

"If ya had the phone number, ya might get online with one 'em directory services. I think if ya got a phone number, ya can plug it in and get the address."

"How the hell ya know stuff like that, Jack? Ya done gone hi-tech on me, or what?"

"You got a computer, don't ya?"

"Hell yeah. . .never did figger out how to work the damned thing, though. *She* done it all for me. And that's another thing! She got all my accounts put into that damned thing, and now I can't figure out none of it. Thought them things was supposed to be logical, but I reckon if they are, then *I ain't.*"

"Logical. . .hey that reminds me of a joke." Jack began laughing and slapped Kirby on the back. "Ya heard the one 'bout the two rednecks that decided to go off to college?"

"Nah. That don't sound too logical in itself, though—two rednecks going off to college, I mean." They both laughed.

"Yeah, guess ya got a point there, Kirb. That's what makes this so funny, though. Anyhow, Bubba and ole Billy Bob, they decided they weren't gettin' nowhere in life, ya see, so they figured it might he'p to get 'em some college. Well, when they get there, Bubba, he meets first with this fellow calls hisself an advisor, to try and figger out what courses he oughta be takin'. The professor, he begins telling ole Bubba that he's gonna have to take some math, and definitely a English course or two, and of course, logic.

"Logic, whut's that?" asked ole Bubba.

"Well, son, let me see if I can explain," the professor said. "Do you own a weedeater?"

"Yeah, shore, why?"

"Well, then, it follows that you *must* have a yard."

"Yeah, course I got a yard...so?"

"And if you have a yard, then that means you must have a house."

"Yeah—well, a trailer. . .but how the hell did you figger that out?"

Now suddenly ole Bubba, he's beginning to see what that professor meant about that logic. He thinks it's pretty good stuff, being able to figure things out that way.

The professor continued, "And if you have a house, then maybe you have a wife or a girlfriend, right?"

"Well, yeah—uh...we ain't married, but—"

"And if you have a girlfriend, then that means you must be heterosexual."

"You mean. . .Well, hell yes! Damned straight! Course I am!"

"So, you see how you can apply logic to figure things out."

"Well, I'll be damned! Reckon you'n fer shore sign me up fer that there logic course."

Ole Bubba, he finishes his meeting with the adviser and goes and finds his buddy, Billy Bob, who says, "Well, Bubba, what'd he tell ya to take?"

"Said I oughta take me some math, a English course, and of course, *logic*."

"Logic? What the hell's *logic*, Bubba?"

"Well, let's see. . .lemme see if I'n explain it to ya sorta like he done to me. See, here's how that there logic works, Billy Bob. First, ya see, I gotta ask ya if ya got a weedeater"

"Huh? A weedeater?"

"Yeah, that's what I said, a *weedeater*. You got one?"

"Hell no, you know damned well I ain't got no weedeater, Bubba—ain't got no yard, so why'd I need me a weedeater?"

"Well, see, that's what I mean. That's how this logic works, ya see..."

"Hell no, I don't see!"

"Well, *logically*—at least accordin' to what that feller just told me—that there proves that yer a queer."

Jack and Kirby laughed so hard that Kirby had to go take a leak. When he came back, he said, "That was pretty good, Jack. Now tell me some more 'bout how that there logic works—I mean about the computer stuff."

"Well, I don't know much about it, actually, but my brother-in-law, he's a big computer nerd. He was showin' me once when I was over at his place how you'n get online and find out all kinds a stuff. See, he puts in this phone number for somebody lives out there in Cali-forn-ya, and about two seconds later, hell, their address just popped right up on the screen, sorta like magic."

"Hmmm. . .that right?"

"That's right. So see, if ya could find out the phone number, ya could prob'bly get the address, no sweat."

Kirby took a long swig of his beer and thought about it for a minute. "Okay, maybe I'll look through some of the old phone bills—assuming I'n find where the bitch filed 'em, that is. Ya really think if I was to give ya the phone number, ya could have—what's his name, yer brother-in-law?"

"Bruce. Can ya believe it? Sister married a guy named *Bruce! Brucie Lee,* I call him. . .ya know, like from that song them guys made up from *Puff, the Magic Dragon*—ya know, the one they called *Muff, the Tragic Faggot.*"

"Yeah, how's that go anyhow, I forgot?"

"You know, same tune as *Puff, the Magic Dragon*—goes something like this: *Muff, the tragic faggot. . .lived by the sea, and frolicked in the ocean mist with a boy named Brucie Lee.* . .Really gets to ole Brucie when I call him *Brucie Lee.* Course, I always sing him a chorus of that song. Anyway, Ole Brucie, I reckon he's okay, though. . .but I bet he wouldn't last five minutes in here. Know what I mean?"

"Yeah, I reckon that's so. Sure wouldn't mind if a couple of *Brucie's* decided to come in tonight."

"What? You ain't that horny already, are ya?"

"No, asshole! What I mean is, I feel like kicking some butt. How 'bout you?"

"Hell yes! Just like old times, right?"

"Right."

"So, anyway, Kirb, see can ya get me that number and I'll see if ole Brucie can get ya the address."

"Yeah, maybe I'll look around for it—but not today. Tonight this ole boy's plannin' on gettin' drunk, maybe laid—yeah, definitely laid—and like I said, maybe kick some butt. Ready for another Bud?"

"Hell yeah! I'm just getting started. Reckon them broads over yonder in that booth might get to looking pretty good 'fore too much longer, what'd ya think, Kirb? Might hafta kick ole Buck and Bobby Joe's butts first, though. Looks like they done made a move on 'em."

"Hell, that wouldn't be no problem! We could do that with one hand tied behind our backs, right? We done cleaned up lots bigger bad boys than them two jerks."

"Yeah, I reckon that's true. Well, drink up, ole buddy. Then maybe we'll go over and give it a shot. Suzie-Floozie, bring us two more!"

Chapter 9

Clara Wilson had been looking out her window every few minutes since daybreak, hoping to see the little girl. She got excited earlier when she saw Carter backing the Ford Explorer out of his driveway. When she saw him look back and wave, she glanced toward the front porch and was surprised to see Jenny sitting out there in her wheelchair, waving goodbye to her grandfather. Hoping the little girl might be out there for a while, Clara quickly located one of her cutest kittens, a tawny tabby that had been born in a litter just a few weeks ago. She tucked the kitten under her arm and set out toward the Carter house, ole Gordy, the big German shepherd, ambling along behind her.

The little girl looked up as the old lady approached, squinted her eyes against the bright morning sun, and said, "Hello, who're you?"

"Why, I'm Clara. Don't you know me?"

"No ma'am, I don't think so."

"Well, I know you. You're Jenny. Don't you remember me?"

The old woman stared at the little girl, unable to understand why Jenny didn't recognize her. With her knobby fingers, she stroked the kitten she carried in her arms, awaiting the little girl's reply.

Jenny screwed up her face, cocked her head and flashed the old woman a puzzled look. "How do you know my name?"

"Why, your name's Jenny. Same as always."

The little girl stared at the kitten the old lady held in her arms. "What's your kitty's name?"

"Oh, this here's Amanda. I know ya always liked kittens, Jenny."

"Oh, yes, I love kitties. . .but Mommy won't let me have one."

"Would ya like to hold her?"

"Yes, could I?"

"Sure. She looks just like that kitten ya used to have when . . ." Clara stared off into the distance for a few moments, then added, "Well, I guess ya don't remember."

The old lady carefully handed the kitten to Jenny, who smiled and placed it across her knees. She rubbed her hand down its back and the kitten purred, seeming perfectly content to curl up on the little girl's lap and allow her to stroke it.

The old lady smiled. "You here by yerself, Jenny?"

"No, ma'am, Mommy's inside. Ole Pa's gone to see 'bout Mommy's car—she wrecked it, ya know. I got hurt in the wreck and I have to stay in this wheelchair now."

"Yes, I know about that."

Jenny held up her new doll. "See my new Barbie that Ole Pa and Mommy got me for my birthday. My others were in the wreck. I hope none of them was hurt. Ole Pa's gonna see about them today. I hope he finds them and they're okay."

"Barbie? That your baby's name?"

"Huh?"

"Your baby? It's name's Barbie?"

"Uh-huh."

"I got names for all my babies, too."

"This is my new *Princess* Barbie. I had two other Barbies—I hope they're okay. . .and a Ken too—ya know, Barbie's boyfriend."

"Hmmm. Three babies all named Barbie. How do ya tell 'em apart?"

"Oh, that's easy. See, Princess Barbie wears this princess outfit. . .and her hair's all done up and she has this hat with diamonds all over it?"

"Yes, I see. Barbie, huh?"

"Uh-huh."

"Funny name for babies."

"Do you live nearby?"

"Oh, yes, I live just right over there," Clara said, pointing toward her house.

"Oh, so you're the lady that's got all them dogs and cats?"

"Yes, that's right. They're my babies. I got names for them all, too. Gordy, here, he's my favorite. . .but he's gonna die soon. Ya like dogs, Jenny?"

Gordy had moved onto the porch and was lying in the sun next to Jenny's wheelchair. Jenny reached down and petted him on the head.

"Yes, ma'am, but I like kitties better."

"Ya do, huh? Would ya like to keep her?"

"Ya mean . . ."

"Sure, you'n keep her if ya wanna."

Jenny looked down at the kitten and stroked its tiny head. "Really! I like her a lot. But I'd have to ask Mommy. She'll probably say *no*—she always does."

"Well, just let me know later, then."

"Okay, I will."

"Being in that wheelchair, it's not so bad, is it?"

"No, ma'am, I don't mind so much. But Mommy and Ole Pa, they think it's awful. They don't understand why I can't walk."

"Well, I know 'bout people not understanding. Yes, indeed, I know 'bout that."

"Are you the old lady they say's *crazy*. . .the one who walks around at night?"

"Who told ya that, child?"

"Uh, well, uh. . .I heard there's this lady who goes walking, sometimes in the middle of the night. Ole Pa says she's a nice lady, though, but that people just don't understand and some thinks she's crazy."

"Is that what he says? Well, I reckon some folks thinks I'm crazy, all right. Do you think I'm crazy, Jenny?"

"No ma'am. . .I think you're nice."

"Well, now. Perhaps all those folk might just be mistaken, then. What'd ya think, Jenny?"

"Yes, ma'am, I bet they are. What did you say your name is?"

"My name? Why, my name's Clara."

"Clara? Clara who? My Mommy says I shouldn't never call older people by their first names."

"Well, I reckon that might be so, Jenny. But I guess it's all right if they tell ya that ya can. You'n call me Clara. It'll be all right."

"Okay, uh, Clara. Can I really have the kitty?"

"Course ya can. Didn't I say ya could?"

"Yes, ma'am, but . . ."

"But what, child?"

"But what if Mommy and Ole Pa won't let me keep her? I know they won't!"

"Oh, I bet they will. You just tell 'em Clara said ya could. Said it was your birthday, didn't ya?"

"Uh-huh. I just turned eight years old."

"Well, then, Happy Birthday, Jenny. You'n keep the kitten for your birthday present from me."

"Thank you, Clara."

"You're welcome, child. Your grandfather, he give me a birthday present once. Know what it was?"

"Uh-uh."

"Give me a nice new flashlight. Don't know how he knew it was my birthday, though. Nice man, your grandfather."

"Yes, ma'am, he sure is." Jenny smiled at the old woman and added, "I like you, Clara. I don't think you're crazy at all."

"Well, thank ya, child. Some folks just don't understand, I reckon."

"Yes ma'am, I reckon that's sure the truth."

"Maybe ya'd like to come over sometime and see my other babies. I got lots of dogs and cats."

"Oh, uh, okay, I guess so."

Suddenly the front door opened and Patty came out onto the porch. She looked first at the old lady, then at her daughter and then down at the kitten that lay purring in Jenny's lap.

"Hi Mommy. This is Clara. She's nice."

"Hello, Clara. I'm Patty, Jenny's mother. How are you?"

"Tolerable, I guess. Jenny here wants to keep the kitten. Reckon it's all right. Give it to her for her birthday."

"Uh, well, I. . .I suppose—if it's okay with her Ole Pa." Patty again looked down at the kitten, then back at the old lady. "That's mighty nice of you, Clara."

"Ah, it ain't no trouble. I got a bunch more. Let her keep it. She likes it, and as ya'n see, it likes her."

"Yes, I can see that. Well, I suppose it'll be all right. But I'll have to check with Dad."

"Oh, he won't mind. I know these things. Little girls needs a kitten."

"Yes, well, you may be right. Thank you, Clara. But I'll still have to check with him, and I'll have to think about it."

"Please, Mommy. Can I keep her? Pleeease."

"We'll see, Jenny."

After a few moments of silence, the old lady said, "Meant to be, I reckon. Little girls needs a kitten. Reminds me, I gotta go see 'bout my other babies. Jenny, take real good care of Amanda now, ya hear?"

"Yes, ma'am, I will. Thank you, Clara. Bye."

"Goodbye, child. Good day to ya, lady."

"Goodbye, Clara. Thanks for the kitten. I'm sure it'll make Jenny happy. You sure you want to give it to her?"

"Wouldn't a done it if I wasn't sure," the old lady replied. She then turned and ambled toward her house. Old Gordy struggled to his feet and trailed along behind.

When Clara Wilson was gone, Jenny said, "Mommy, she don't seem like a crazy lady to me. She seems nice. Is she really crazy like they say?"

"I don't know, Jenny. I guess maybe she's just a little different. Ole Pa says she doesn't mean anyone any harm. But Jenny, I don't want you being around her, especially when you're alone."

"Why not, Mommy? I like Clara."

"I know, sweetie, but she. . .you just never know what she might do."

"What'd ya mean?"

"I don't know. I mean, you just stay away from her, okay Jenny? I'm afraid she just. . .well, Ole Pa says sometimes she just doesn't know what she's doing."

"She seemed okay to me."

"Yes, I know, Jenny. I suppose sometimes she is, but other times. . .well, Ole Pa says she...I just don't want you spending time around her, Jenny, especially if me or Ole Pa's not around."

"Okay, Mommy. But I think Clara's a nice lady."

"Yes, I'm sure she is. But you remember what I told you."

"Okay, but I think maybe she just needs a friend."

"A friend? Well, maybe so."

"Maybe I could be her friend, Mommy."

"I don't know, Jenny. I don't think so. But we'll see. You just remember what I said, though. If you're outside and she comes over, you call me or Ole Pa, okay?"

"Okay, Mommy."

Jenny looked down at the kitten and smiled. "I like Amanda. Isn't she cute, Mommy?"

"Yes, she is. Come on, sweetie. I'll push you and your kitty—"

"Her name's Amanda!"

"Oh, okay. I'll push you and Amanda back inside. I bet you're about ready for some lunch. Ole Pa should be home soon with our clothes and things. Then maybe we'll give you a nice hot bath and you can put on your new jeans and that nice yellow sweater I got you for your birthday."

"Okay, Mommy." Jenny looked down at the kitten. "Can Amanda take a bath with me?"

Patty smiled. "We'll see, sweetheart. I don't think kittens much like water, though. Maybe she can just sit and watch while you have a bath."

As she was pushing Jenny back inside, Patty glanced toward the Wilson house and noticed the old woman standing in her yard, staring at them. An eerie feeling swept through Patty, causing her to shiver. She hurried inside and closed the door. Something about that old woman frightened her, although she couldn't pinpoint exactly what it was.

Chapter 10

During the first few days Jenny was home, Patty and I attempted to settle into a routine for taking care of her every need. I built a small ramp on the end of the front porch nearest the driveway so Jenny could come and go through the front door instead of the garage. I still found it strange that she didn't seem as concerned about her injury as I had expected she might be—certainly not as much as her mother and I were. She hardly smiled anymore, though, and sometimes her eyes betrayed a kind of sadness that I had never before noticed in the normally bright-eyed little girl. Only when she was playing with her new kitten did she seem her old self. I thought about how I might feel if I were in Jenny's position, having undergone that kind of trauma and now uncertain if she would ever walk again. Under the circumstances, she was doing rather well, I concluded.

The first physical therapy session and doctor's visit were scheduled for this afternoon. Patty dressed Jenny in the new purple warm-up suit she had bought for her to wear during the therapy sessions. Purple was Jenny's favorite color and she looked both cute and comfortable in the soft matching cotton pants and jacket. The doctor's appointment was scheduled first, at one-thirty in the afternoon, followed by the therapy session at three o'clock. They planned to stop at McDonalds for lunch on the way, so at eleven-fifteen, we decided it was time we get ready to leave.

Jenny began shaking her head. "No, I don't wanna go. I don't wanna. Please don't make me." Tears came into her eyes.

"But sweetheart, we have to take you to the doctor and for your first physical therapy session," Patty pleaded. "I bet that'll be fun. There's nothing to be afraid of. They're just going to help you learn to use your legs again."

"No, I don't wanna. I don't wanna go, Mommy! Please don't make me."

Patty squatted in front of her daughter. "What are you afraid of, sweetheart? They're not going to give you a shot or anything like that. The doctor just wants to take a look at your legs and back and—"

"No, that's not. . .it's not that, Mommy."

"Then what? What is it, sweetheart?"

"I—I just don't wanna go. . .I don't wanna leave kitty alone, Mommy."

"Oh, I'm sure she'll be fine, sweetie. We won't be gone that long."

"Please, Mommy. Please. . .I don't wanna go."

"Sweetheart, what is it? What are you afraid of? The doctor?"

"No! I'm just scared."

Jenny began sobbing and Patty took her into her arms. "Sweetheart, there's nothing to be scared about. No one's going to hurt you."

"It's not that, Mommy. I'm just afraid. . ."

"Are you afraid to get back into a car again, Jenny?"

Jenny nodded her head. "Uh-huh. Please don't make me, Mommy. I'm so scared."

"Sweetie, there's no other way we can get to the hospital. Ole Pa's going to drive, and you know he's a really *good* driver. Look outside. . .it's nice and sunny. . .no fog. I understand your reluctance, sweetheart—I mean, I'm a little scared myself every time I get in a car now. . .but there really is no other choice. So come on, what'd ya say? Let's go now so we have time to stop at McDonalds on the way. Aren't you hungry?"

"I guess so," Jenny said, sniffling and turning away.

I had worried that Jenny might be afraid to ride in a car again—I imagined I might feel the same way—but this was our first indication of any reluctance from her. She hadn't seemed to be bothered during the ride home from the hospital a few days ago, yet apparently now that she'd thought about it, she was developing some sort of phobia. I wondered what we should do, remembering the old adage about when a person falls off a horse, they should get right back on; otherwise, they might be afraid of horses for the rest of their lives. Should they force Jenny to face her fear now or should they reschedule the appointments for another day and try to ease her into the concept of riding in a car again? Probably it wouldn't matter, though; at some point she would have to face getting into a car again, so it might just as well be now.

I backed the Explorer out of the garage so there would be more room to load the wheelchair, while Patty pushed Jenny out through the front door, across the porch and down the ramp to the driveway. When I opened the door for Patty to help Jenny into the vehicle, Jenny began screaming and shaking her head.

"Noooo! Noooo! Please, Mommy. Don't make me do it. Don't make me do it. Don't make me do it." Over and over, she kept repeating, "Don't make me do it," the words coming in shorter and shorter gasps until she finally ran out of breath.

Catching her breath, Jenny then looked at me and pleaded, "Ole Pa, pleeease. Don't make me." She then put her face in her hands and began sobbing.

Patty tried to comfort her daughter, but Jenny shoved her away and turned her face toward the back of the wheelchair. Shivers ran through her body, as she wrenched with sobs. I didn't know what to do, but knew I had to do something, so I went over to the wheelchair, squatted beside Jenny and took her hand.

"It's okay, sweetheart. Don't cry. Here, let me push you back onto the porch. We don't have to go now, if you don't want to."

When Jenny was back on the front porch, Patty came over, took Jenny in her arms and held her while the little girl sobbed. After a few moments, Patty said, "Sweetie, it's okay. I know how you feel. It's okay. You don't have to do this right now. We'll wait. Can we talk about it? Okay?"

Jenny glanced up at her mother and mumbled between sobs, "I—I guess so. But Mommy, I. . .I'm really scared."

"I know, darling. Mommy's a little scared too. But you can't continue the rest of your life without ever riding in a car again. And we have to take you to see Doctor Greenfield. You like him, remember. Then we'll go meet the nice person who's going to help you learn to walk again. How about it, Jenny? Shall we give it a try? What'd you say?"

Jenny didn't say anything for a few moments. Patty and I exchanged worried looks. Neither of us spoke, as Jenny seemed to be considering the matter.

Finally, Jenny looked up, folded her arms across her chest and screwed her face into a look of firm determination. "Okay, but I'm *only* going if Amanda can go too!" Then she squeezed her eyes shut, as if settling the matter.

I looked at Patty and nodded. "Okay, sweetheart," Patty agreed. "I think that'll be okay. We'll have to leave the kitten in the car while we go in to see the doctor, though. Shall I get one of your little blankets to keep her warm?"

Jenny opened her eyes, pushed out her lower lip and sniffled. "Okay," she feebly replied.

Patty went inside and came back out with the kitten wrapped in Jenny's favorite blue blanket. She handed the bundle to Jenny, who held it in her arms as she might have held a baby. I helped Jenny into the backseat of the car and she sat with eyes closed, squeezing the bundled kitten to her breast.

Patty opened the back door on the other side. "Would you like Mommy to ride in the back with you?"

"Uh-huh," Jenny answered softly, keeping her eyes shut tightly.

Patty climbed in beside her daughter and fastened each of their seatbelts. As I backed slowly out of the driveway, Jenny moved closer to her mother and rested her head on her shoulder. She kept her eyes closed and by the time we were down the mountain, Jenny was fast asleep, her kitten curled up on her chest, purring softly.

A nurse had already assisted Jenny onto the examination table and she was lying there flat of her back when Doctor Greenfield walked into the examination room. He didn't seem quite so harried as he had the last time they'd seen him. He looked down at Jenny, smiled warmly and said, "Well, young lady, how're you feeling today?"

"Okay, I guess. . .I got a kitty."

"A kitty. How nice. What's your kitty's name?"

"Amanda."

"Amanda, what a pretty name."

"I didn't name her, though."

"Oh?"

"Clara did."

"I see. Well, let's have a look at you, Jenny. That's a mighty pretty outfit you're wearing. I'm going to push up your pant legs a little so I can feel you legs, okay? Let me know if you feel anything where I touch you."

Doctor Greenfield squeezed Jenny's legs in several places, ending up at her feet where he wiggled her toes and then tickled the bottom of her foot. Jenny didn't flinch or move until he tickled her foot, then she giggled.

"Can you feel that, Jenny?" the doctor asked.

"I can feel you tickling my foot, but I still can't move it."

"Good! That's an improvement. I'm going to touch your feet in a few places now with this needle. But don't worry, I won't stick you hard. Tell me each time if you can feel a prick."

First, the doctor lightly touched the needle to the bottom of Jenny's right foot. She didn't move, but told him that she could sort of feel it. Then he poked her gently in various places around the bottoms and tops of both feet. She said she could feel the needle prick a little, but that she still couldn't move her legs or feet. Next, the doctor took a small rubber mallet and tapped Jenny's knees, ankles and the tops of her feet in a several places.

Finally finished with his examination, the doctor pulled a stool over and sat across from Patty and me. "There seems to be some slight improvement in her reflexes. And as you could see, she's regained some feeling in her feet and legs. That's good news. This is about what we expected at this point. It will probably take a few sessions of physical therapy before she's able to begin moving her legs again."

Turning to Jenny, the doctor said, "What I'd like you to do for me, young lady, is to let your mommy rub your legs for you every night before you go to sleep, and again the next morning when you wake up. That will help maintain circulation. We don't want all your muscles to get lazy now, do we? I think you're going to be walking again real soon. After we finish here, I'd like to get another picture. You remember that funny sounding machine we moved across you when you were here before, don't you?"

"Uh-huh. It didn't even hurt."

"That's right. Then afterwards you can go over and meet your instructor in the PT lab. I think you'll like physical therapy. It's sort of like a gym where they have all kinds of special machines, such as stationary bicycles that you can ride to help you learn to move your legs again. How does that sound, Jenny?"

"Okay, I guess. Can I see the picture you take of my bones?"

"Sure. You'll be able to watch it on a little TV monitor right when it's happening. You just tell the technician that I said it was okay."

"Okay." Jenny then screwed up her face and asked, "How can I ride a bicycle if I can't move my legs?"

"Oh, that's easy, Jenny," Doctor Greenfield explained. "See, this is a special bicycle. It moves all by itself. You can control it with your arms and hands and it will move your legs for you. I bet it'll be lots of fun." Turning to Patty and Tom, the doctor asked, "Do either of you have any questions?"

They looked at each other, then Patty looked back at the doctor and asked, "How long do you think it'll be before—I mean, how much time are we looking at here, Doctor? I can't continue to stay here indefinitely. At some point, I have to think about going back to work. And we need to get Jenny back in school."

Jenny began shaking her head. "No...I don't wanna go back, Mommy. I wanna stay with Ole Pa. Please, Mommy, don't make me go back. Pleeease."

Doctor Greenfield patted Jenny on the head. "Don't worry, young lady. I don't think you'll be going anywhere for a while yet—not until we have you up and walking again." He then looked at Patty and Tom. "I wish I could tell you what kind of time we're looking at here, but it would only be a guess. These things vary, case by case, and we really have no way of determining exactly how long her recovery will take. I can tell you that statistically these kinds of injuries usually take somewhere between three weeks and six months."

Patty grimaced and the doctor smiled and quickly added, "Usually it's closer to weeks than months, though." He then looked at Jenny, who appeared to be listening intently. "A lot depends on this young lady. If she works really hard and does all her exercises, which I'm sure she will, I think we'll see amazing progress. She looks like a real fighter to me, so I expect to see her up and around in no time. I want to see you back here in a week, young lady—and wiggling those toes next time. Okay, Jenny?"

After a series of X-rays, Patty and I pushed Jenny across the parking lot to the building containing the physical therapy department. As soon as we were inside the door, a handsome young black man approached. He was dressed in white utility pants and shirt and he displayed a wide grin.

He looked down at Jenny and his grin widened even more. "So, who we have here, *mon*? Let me see—I think this must be. . .hmmm. . .Jenny, right? How ya doing today, Jenny?"

The young man spoke in a singsong accent prevalent in people from one of the Caribbean islands; probably Jamaica, I guessed. He pronounced the word man as *mon*, and sprinkled the word throughout his speech, whether appropriate or not.

"Okay, I guess," Jenny replied. "How'd ya know my name?"

Tony's smile broadened. "Magic, *mon*. My name's Tony. You and me, we gonna have us lots of fun today, Jenny. We gonna learn to use all these fancy machines, take you for rides like you never had before, *mon*. This maybe not jus' like Disney World, but close. . .veeery close. What you think, Jenny?"

"Uh, I dunno."

"All much fun. You see. When you are ready, we begin. You are *good* looking chick, *mon*."

Jenny was smiling already at the young man's accent and upbeat attitude. Patty and I looked at each other, smiled and nodded, agreeing that this part of Jenny's recovery process was probably going to go well. Obviously, Tony was great with children and there was no doubt he enjoyed his job.

Tony then turned to us and said, "You people's gonna hafta go now. We don't allow no big folks in here while we be playing, *mon*. Me and Jenny, we gonna have us some fun for about forty-five minutes. You come on back then, okay *mon*?"

When we arrived later to pick up Jenny, she was giggling and seemed to be having a great time.

Tony greeted us with a big smile. "You promise, you bring Jenny back really, really soon, *mon*. We get to do this twice a week, right Jenny? So, I gonna be seeing you same time on Thursday, okay *mon*?"

As they put Jenny into her wheelchair and took her out to the car, she was bubbling with enthusiasm, explaining all about the machines and how much fun it had been and how much she liked Tony. "He's soooo nice. He's from a King's town down on some island called *Ja-may-go* in the *Carry-bean* Sea."

Jenny seemed so keyed up about her new adventure that she didn't even protest this time when they helped her into the car. They found kitty rolled up in the blanket, sound asleep, and Jenny picked her up like a baby, placed her against her chest and the kitten began purring. Soon Jenny and kitty were both fast asleep.

As we turned into my driveway, I noticed something lying on the front porch. As I got closer, I realized it was a large dog. It looked like that big German shepherd from next door. Strange, the dog wasn't reacting to the noise of our arrival. I stopped before pulling into the garage and Patty and I helped Jenny out of the car and into her wheelchair. Jenny held kitty in her lap as Patty pushed the little wheelchair up the ramp and onto the porch. The old dog still didn't move.

I pulled the Explorer into the garage, then came out and walked across the porch to where Patty stood, staring down at the immobile animal.

"Mommy! It's Gordy!" announced Jenny. "Can I pet him?"

"Not now, sweetheart. I think he's, uh, taking a nap. Let's not bother him now, okay?"

Patty raised her gaze to her father and silently mouthed, "I think he's dead." Then she hurriedly pushed Jenny on into the house.

Nudging the animal with my foot, I confirmed Patty's assumption. Glancing toward the Wilson house, I saw the old lady standing in her side yard, watching our every move.

Chapter 11

Kirby awoke, his body aching in places he'd forgotten he even had. His head pounded as if some big guy with a sledgehammer was marching around inside, banging on his skull, trying to get out. When he rolled over in bed, he found that he hurt in even more places. He tried to remember why his body might be aching like this. Vaguely, he recalled that he and Jack had drunk a lot of beer the night before and that at some point they had gone over to make a move on those bitches who'd been in that corner booth. First they'd had to dispose of Buck and Bobby Joe, though, which must not have turned out as easy as they had expected. He guessed they must have gotten the job done, though, since he noticed one of the women was here in his bed now.

Damn, she's ugly. Must've been drunker than I realized.

The woman was lying there snoring loudly enough to wake the dead, which was probably what had awakened him, Kirby decided. He punched her in the ribs and she rolled over and moaned, but was soon snoring again. Kirby looked more closely at her and experienced the same remorse that usually befell him whenever he made a midnight move on a broad who earlier in the evening had not looked so inviting. As was invariably the case, this morning she was repulsive, lying there on her side, her portly cellulite-ridden flanks taking up half his bed. Kirby couldn't remember what they had done last night, but hoped it had been nothing. Realizing he had to get rid of her before he became physically sick, he put his foot on her fat behind and shoved her halfway off the bed.

"What the hell! Leave me alone. Wanna sleep."

"Sleeping's over, woman! Up and at 'em. I got work to do." He shoved her with his foot again and she slid off onto the floor with a loud thud.

"Dammit! Why'd ya do that? Where's your bathroom?"

Kirby pointed toward the door and the woman got up, pulled a rumpled sheet around her gross, naked body and staggered out the door. Kirby hoped he hadn't done what he feared he probably had last night. How could he be so stupid?

By the time the woman returned, Kirby had pulled on his jeans and a grungy T-shirt. He glanced at her again and thought he might become sick as she slowly pulled her dress over her head and down over that massive, flabby body. She certainly looked lots older this morning than he seemed to remember from last night. Must have been all that makeup and the dim lights, he reasoned, looking away and forcing himself not to look at her again until she was fully dressed. Then he handed her a twenty-dollar bill and said, "Phone's in the living room. Get in there and call yourself a taxi."

Later, after several cups of strong coffee, Kirby fumbled through the desk drawers in his cluttered office, unable to make heads or tails of the filing system Patty had devised. The more he looked, the angrier he became. His head still ached, although more from a hangover than anything else, he decided. Other than a bruise below his left eye, he didn't look nearly as bad as he'd anticipated he might. He tried to remember what the other guy might have looked like afterwards, but the images were only fleeting. He hoped his buddy, Jack, was all right this morning. Probably he would be, Kirby decided, since Jack usually had no problem taking care of himself, whether drinking or fighting. During the first few years after high school, Kirby and Jack had gone out night after night, moving from bar to bar, just looking for a good fight; usually they found at least one.

Kirby couldn't find a single telephone bill. Where the hell could she have filed them? Finally, exasperated to the point of desperation, he pulled all the drawers out of his desk and began dumping the contents onto the floor. Nothing he saw looked like a phone bill. From the looks of things, he needed to clean out the drawers anyway, though. Then he turned back to the file cabinet and looked through those drawers again. Finally, in a folder labeled Bell South, he found them. *Bell South*? Now why the hell didn't she just file them under Telephone or Phone or Bills Paid? He would never understand the way women think.

Pulling out a handful of statements, Kirby spread them out on his desk and scanned them for a few moments. On last year's November statement, he noticed a number he didn't recognize. The statement listed a long distance call to area code 828. Kirby seldom made long distance phone calls, so this must be a call she'd made to her old man. He looked through a few other statements and found records of three other calls to the same number. Since he didn't see any other long distance calls listed, this had to be it. Damn, the woman had talked a long time during one of those calls, running up a bill of $9.54. Small wonder his business wasn't doing too well.

Kirby wrote down the number and tried to remember if he and Jack had agreed to meet again tonight at the Red Dog. Probably they had, he decided. Jack would likely be there anyway, so maybe Kirby could give him the phone number tonight. He didn't hold much hope that this would yield an address, though. Kirby considered this Internet stuff a worthless, nerdy fad that would soon go away. But what the hell? It wouldn't hurt to give it a shot. Maybe he would get lucky.

Chapter 12

The old lady continued to watch as I rolled the old dog's carcass off the porch and into a wheelbarrow, which I then began pushing over toward her house. She met me at her front gate. All of her other dogs were barking and running back and forth along the fence, jumping and acting as if they wanted to attack me. I was thankful I didn't have to try to proceed into the old lady's yard without her there to protect him—at least, I hoped she could protect me.

"Knew he was gonna go soon. Sorry it happened on your porch, Carter."

"It's okay, Mrs. Wilson. I'm sorry he died. What do you want me to do with him? If you'd like, I'd be glad to help you bury him."

"Done got the grave dug. Round back near the edge of the bluff. Been knowing he was going soon, so I dug it a few days ago. Reckon ya might just wheel him on around there for me, if ya don't mind. I'll be saying a few words and then I'll put him in his resting-place. I'd like to do this alone, though, so if you'll just put him on the ground there beside the grave, I'll handle it from there on. I sure appreciate your bringing him over."

"No problem. Glad to do it. If you'll just show me where you want him."

"Right around this way."

The old lady headed around the side of her house toward the bluff, and I followed. Laying the wheelbarrow on its side next to the hole Clara Wilson had dug, I gently rolled the old dog's body out onto the ground. I marveled at the grave, which looked as if professional gravediggers had prepared it. I wondered how she'd had the strength to dig a hole of such proportions. The grave was about four feet long by two feet wide and perhaps three feet deep. The sides were straight and even, as if measured by a carpenter's square. Dirt from the hole lay in a neat pile on one side, and the old lady had already erected a marker in the shape of a cross, made from two pieces of board fastened together. Scratched onto the board across the top was the word, *Gordy*. When I looked at the old woman, I noticed her intense sadness and a tear came into my eye.

Turning quickly away, I said, "Anything else I can do to help, Mrs. Wilson?"

"No, that'll be fine. Thank you, Carter."

"No problem, Clara. Glad to do it."

"Tell Jenny I said take good care of that kitten."

"I will, and thank you again. She loves that kitten. Hardly lets it out of her sight. I think it's about the best thing that's happened to her lately. That was mighty thoughtful of you."

"Weren't no problem. Little girls needs a kitten. That's what I always say. Well, good day, Carter."

After pushing the wheelbarrow back to my house, I went around to the side facing away from the Wilson house, and for several minutes I sprayed the inside of the wheelbarrow with a water hose.

Leaving the wheelbarrow out in the sun to dry, I went inside. Jenny was taking a nap, so Patty and I sat out in the room overlooking the bluff while I told her about the grave the old lady had dug and that she was planning on conducting some sort of weird ceremony. We could barely see her through the window as she set about performing the task of burying the old dog.

"That's weird. She's really crazy, isn't she, Dad?"

"Well, I don't know, Patty. She just loves her animals, I guess. Sometimes she seems fairly normal, but at other times, it seems her mind is off someplace else. I have that problem myself sometimes. I call it having a *senior moment*. Heard someone say the other day that their *screen saver* just came on. Guess part of it's just old age. Clara may be a bit senile, but I don't know if I think she's actually crazy—whatever that means."

"Well, I don't want Jenny around her much, and certainly not alone. You do agree, don't you?"

"Oh, I suppose so. But I don't think she'd ever hurt Jenny. She seems to feel some sort of special attachment to her, almost as if . . ."

"As if?"

"I don't know. Maybe she. . .well, I heard she had a daughter. I guess she'd be about my age now. I've never seen her come around, though, and the old lady never talks about her. Who knows, maybe Jenny reminds her of her own daughter. . .you know, when she was a little girl."

"Hmmm. . .maybe so. That's a little scary, don't you think?"

"Oh, maybe a little. . .but I don't think it'll cause any problem."

"Maybe not, but I wish there was some way we could keep the old lady from just showing up whenever Jenny's outside. I don't want to have to keep her inside all the time just to keep her away from that crazy old woman."

"I don't think it's going to be a problem, Patty."

"Well, I hope you're right, Dad."

"She sure seemed sad to be burying that old dog. Guess he was one of her favorites. Don't know how she keeps up with them all. Must be at least thirty more over there."

"I can't see why anyone would want that many animals," Patty said, glancing back toward the Wilson house. "There's no way she can care for them all. Looks like she has enough trouble just taking care of herself. Someone should call the health department, or something. I can imagine what the inside of her house must look like—and smell like, too. Didn't you say she has several cats she keeps inside?"

"Yeah, a bunch, I've heard. I've never been inside, but I can imagine how bad it must be. I think some of the other neighbors have talked with the health department or the humane society about the situation. Not sure what came of it, though. I'd just as soon stay out of it, myself. Guess I feel kind of sorry for the old lady, and don't want to do anything to hurt her."

"Well, I wouldn't want to get involved either," Patty said, and then was silent for a while, staring off into the valley. Then she turned to her father. "What am I going to do, Dad?"

"What'd you mean?"

"I mean, I can't stay here. . .but I can't leave, either. . .at least, not now. And I really have no place to go, anyway."

"Patty, you'll just have to take things a day at a time, I guess. You know you can stay here as long as you like."

"I know, Dad. . .and thanks."

"I don't think it'd be wise to consider moving Jenny. Not until. . .I mean, well, she seems to like that guy, Tony, and Doctor Greenfield too. You wouldn't want to consider changing doctors in midstream, so I guess you'll just have to stay here until she recovers. I know you want your own life, but we have to think of what's best for Jenny, too."

Patty wiped her eyes with her sleeve. "Yes, Dad, I know that," she said curtly. "I guess you're right, though. We just have to take things one day at a time."

"That's about all I can think to do."

We sat in silence for a few moments, then Patty said, "Oh, the insurance guy called back while you were out."

"Yeah? What'd he say?"

"He said they've agreed to total the car. I'm glad. I never wanted to have to see it again. I could never drive it again, anyway."

"Yeah, I understand, Patty. Are they going to send you a check soon so you can get another car?"

"He said it should be in the mail within a couple of days. You know, the old *the check's in the mail* ploy. Guess I need to go car shopping pretty soon, huh? That's not something I'm looking forward to."

"Only when you're ready. You know you can use my car anytime you want. I don't go many places anyway, so don't worry about it. But I know you want your own car, so we'll go find you a new one whenever you like. Are you planning on getting another Caravan?"

"I don't know, Dad. They're handy, especially with kids. I'm still upset about that damned door coming open, though."

"Well, I suppose that could happen with any car, Patty. That was a pretty bad wreck you had. I think the Caravan's a pretty safe car. You both could've been hurt lots worse, you know."

"Yes, I know. Maybe we'll go shopping in a few days. . .after I get the check. Sure wish I could afford a new car, but I'll just have to get whatever I can buy with the money the insurance pays. They never give you as much as your car's worth, and I sure can't afford a car payment right now."

"Well, don't worry about that, Patty. I can help out a little if necessary. It is my granddaughter who's going to be riding in the car, you know. Can't have her riding around in some old piece of junk. We'll find you a nice car, don't worry."

"Thanks, Dad. I owe you so much already. I really feel bad about all this—imposing on you, and all."

"Well, don't! What else do I have to do with my time and money? Let's just worry about getting Jenny well. We can handle everything else. Okay?"

"Okay, Dad, but—"

Suddenly the front doorbell rang and I got up to answer the door. I found the old lady standing there, tears streaming down her face, dirt all over her hands and clothes.

"Mrs. Wilson, are you all right?"

"It's done. . .came to tell Jenny. . .tell her it's done."

"Well, uh, she's taking a nap right now. Okay if I tell her later?"

"Okay, I guess. It's done. He's gone now. That's all I got to say."

Without another word, the old lady turned and walked away.

Chapter 13

Three days had passed since Kirby had given his friend the old man's phone number. He hadn't expected much, but the more he thought about it, the more he hoped Jack would somehow get that address for him. Although he never wanted to see the woman and her kid again, at the same time, he felt an irresistible urge to find her, teach her that she couldn't get away with just leaving him high and dry like this. He owed her that much, at least, and he wouldn't be satisfied until he had squared his debt. As each day passed, he became angrier about what she'd done to him, until finding her had become an obsession. He would beat the crap out of her and then he'd leave and never have to see or think about her ever again—or her teasing kid, either.

Jack had told Kirby that he would be at the Red Dog tonight, and Kirby was eager as he pulled into the parking lot at around seven o'clock. He looked all around for his buddy's truck, but apparently Jack wasn't there yet. Kirby went inside, flopped onto a barstool and ordered a Bud from Suzie. Suddenly, he wondered why he'd never considered making a move on her. She certainly looked sexy tonight, her flaming red hair tied back in a ponytail and her wearing those tight jeans and a sweater that molded to her body in all the right places. Damn women, they were all the same! Every one of them paraded their wares around, teasing, making men crazy, then holding out to get what they wanted first, after they'd driven the man to the point that he would do nearly anything to get it.

Kirby had never before noticed how big Suzie's boobs were, and found himself fantasizing now about how she would be in the sack. Maybe he would inquire as to what time she got off work tonight. He knew she had the *hots* for him—she'd been obvious about that ever since he starting coming in here again. Strange that until now he hadn't considered taking advantage of what would surely be a fine time. The more he watched her, the hornier he became, until he decided that, assuming ole Jack did get that address for him, he might just ask Suzie to help him celebrate later. He felt a familiar stirring in his groin and his mouth watered just thinking about how it would be.

Kirby was on his second beer when his buddy, Jack, trudged in. Plopping down on the barstool next to Kirby, he looked across the bar toward Suzie and said, "Gimme the usual, Suzie Floozie. You lookin' *good* tonight, woman. Wanna go out later and experience a *real* man?"

Suzie gave him the finger, grabbed a Bud and slid it down the bar. Neither Jack nor Kirby missed her coy smile and the unmistakable twitch of her hip as she turned and went to serve another customer.

Jack slapped Kirby on the back and said, "Hey, ole buddy. Sorry I'm late. Just left ole Brucie's place."

"And?"

"And, well. . .it seems the old man's phone number's unlisted."

"So? What's that mean?"

"Well, according to Brucie Lee, you can't get addresses of numbers that are unpublished."

"Dammit! I knew this was too good to be true. All that damned Internet stuff—waste of time, if ya ask me."

"I'm sorry, Kirb. I wish now I hadn't even mentioned it and got your hopes up."

"Ah, I didn't really expect to get the address this easy anyway. Problem is, now that I've been thinking about this for a few days, I got myself all worked up to the point that now I gotta find that woman and let her know she can't screw up my life this way."

"Ya gonna try to talk her into coming back?"

"Hell no! After I teach her a lesson she'll never forget, then I never wanna see her or her whiny kid ever again. Damned waste of my time. They're more trouble than they're worth and I'm glad they're gone. Still, I gotta slap her around a little before I can let this go. Know what I mean?"

"Hell yes! Can't blame ya there. She sure screwed with the wrong man, I reckon. How the hell ya gonna find the old man's address now, though?"

"I don't know. I thought maybe my good buddy would've helped me out, but I guess if ya want something done right, ya gotta do it yourself."

"I said I'm sorry."

"Ah, it ain't your fault, Jack. I'm just blowing off steam."

"Yeah. . .so, what ya gonna do then, Kirb? Maybe she's not worth the trouble."

"Oh, hell yes! I ain't giving up now. Reckon how big of a area that there area code covers?"

"I dunno. Guess it'd be a pretty fair-sized chunk of real estate," Jack said.

"Yeah, probably. . .but I been thinking. Don't the first three digits of the phone number—what'd ya call 'em, prefixes, or something like that?—don't that sorta narrow down the area some?"

"Yeah, I think maybe you're right. Ya know, that gives me an idea, Kirb. Let me call ole Brucie. He's probably still on his computer—that's about all he ever does when he's home. I told him he oughta get a life, know what I mean? Anyway, lemme call him, see if he can plug this area code in and maybe come up with addresses for some other phone numbers beginning with 828. Maybe that'll give ya some idea where it is. . .or at least narrow it down a little."

"Sounds good to me. Hey Suzie," Kirby yelled. "How 'bout letting my friend here use your phone for a minute."

"Well. . .okay, I guess. Ain't supposed to, but I guess long as it's a local call."

"Oh, hell no! We're gonna call London, England, talk the queen for a bit," Kirby said. "Of course it's a local call, woman! Hey, what time ya get off work tonight, anyhow. Wanna go out and have some *real* fun?"

"In your dreams! Here's the phone. Don't talk long or I'll get'n trouble."

"Okay, thanks, Suzie. Sure could show you a good time, though. Sure ya don't wanna go out?"

She reached across the bar, patted Kirby on the cheek, smiled, winked and said, "Maybe another time, lover boy. I got a boyfriend, ya know."

"So?"

Jack made the call and Bruce said he'd make a quick check on the computer and get right back to him. Kirby ordered another round and he and Jack sat guzzling their beers while they waited. After about ten minutes, the phone rang. Suzie answered, then passed the phone to Jack, who listened for a few moments and hung up.

Kirby stared at his buddy. "Well, what'd he say?"

Jack smiled. "Said he found a bunch of numbers with that area code and prefix. Guess they're all in the western part of the state, mostly around the Asheville area. That narrows it down a little, I reckon."

"Yeah, thanks, Jack. I'm pretty sure it's one 'em little old mountain towns, but there must be bunches of 'em. Now that I think about it, I seem to recall she said it wasn't too far from Asheville. Said she only had to drive a few miles that wasn't freeway."

"Maybe ya oughta just call and talk to her, Kirb. Probably she's just waiting fer ya to call and beg her to come back. That's how they usually want it, ya know. I don't mean ya oughta *beg* her to come back—unless ya want to, of course—but hey, maybe you'n find out where she went if ya was to call her. She'd probably tell ya."

"Hell, she wouldn't never tell me that."

"Nah, I guess not."

Kirby and Jack sat and consumed two more beers each. Then Kirby decided he would go on home, having already given up on waiting until Suzie got off work. She probably wouldn't be worth the wait anyway, he rationalized. Besides, he was tired and he still had to figure out what he was going to do now.

As usual, Kirby had his truck stereo tuned to a classic country station, with the volume set at near maximum. His four speakers, one on each of the doors and two in the back, were powered by a hundred-watt auxiliary amplifier that vibrated the whole truck. As he drove toward his house, he was singing along with Hank Williams Jr., belting out the lyrics to "All my Rowdy Friends Have Settled Down." This song seemed quite appropriate to Kirby as he thought about how he'd settled down himself while *she* was living with him, and now it seemed that most of his rowdy friends weren't around anymore either. Maybe it was time he did settle down. He had to admit he was getting a little old to *get drunk and loud* every night, as the song said. Maybe he ought to find him a good woman and. . .hell, he'd had a good woman—better than he deserved. Why the hell had she left him? He hadn't even screwed around on her during the time she'd been living with him. Well, except for that one time, but he was nearly certain she never found out about that. It had to be the kid, telling her mother a bunch of lies about him.

He was halfway home when the idea came to him in a flash. It seemed so simple that he wondered why he hadn't thought of it before. He almost turned around and went back to tell his buddy, but was afraid Jack might have already left and then Kirby might be tempted to hang around until Suzie got off work, which would probably be at oh-dark-thirty. As he recalled, the place didn't close until around two-thirty a.m.

Kirby continued toward his house, the idea bouncing around in his muddled brain. The more he thought about it the more excited he became. It had to work. Asheville wasn't all that far away. Maybe he could make it over there and back in a half day or so.

By the time he got home, Kirby had decided he was definitely going—maybe even tomorrow, or the next day at the latest.

Chapter 14

Trips to Asheville twice a week for therapy sessions and doctor visits were becoming routine. Jenny seemed even more withdrawn, although she still appeared to enjoy the physical therapy sessions and she and Tony had become best buddies. At home, though, she wouldn't even try to do any of the things the doctor wanted her to do to help strengthen her legs. I was afraid that as time passed her chances of ever walking again would continue to diminish. The doctors had assured us there was no physical reason they could see why Jenny shouldn't be walking by now, and Patty and I frequently discussed the situation while Jenny was taking a nap, which she did nearly every afternoon.

Sometimes, when the weather was warm enough, Jenny liked to sit out on the front porch in the sun, playing with her kitten and her Barbies. Other than her trips to see Tony, this seemed to be her most enjoyable time. Mrs. Wilson sometimes appeared when Jenny was outside on the porch, and this was becoming increasingly disturbing to Patty.

One day Patty met Mrs. Wilson out in the yard and decided to talk to her about her coming around so much. She explained that Jenny needed some time alone, and that she would appreciate it if Clara wouldn't bother Jenny during her play time out on the porch. Tears appeared in the old lady's eyes and she turned and stomped away, her head down. Patty immediately felt awful and wished she hadn't said anything at all. Nevertheless, she just didn't feel right knowing the old lady might be out there with Jenny, filling her head with all kinds of nonsense, and Patty wouldn't even know about it. She didn't want to keep Jenny inside all the time, and no way could someone be out there with her every minute.

Jenny was napping a few days later when I came in from getting the mail. Patty noticed a strange look on her father's face as he stared at a piece of paper he was holding.

"What is it, Dad?"

"Look at this, Patty. It's a note, addressed to Jenny. I guess from Mrs. Wilson."

"What's it say?"

"Well, I can hardly read the scribbling, but it says something like, 'Jenny. Can't see you no more. . .mean woman. . .wanted to tell you . . .' Then there are some words I can't read. It goes on to say something like 'believe in angels. . .watch for angels. . .do what they say.' That's all I can make out."

"That's so weird, Dad. Do you think we should give it to Jenny?"

"I don't know, probably not. Maybe I could just read some of it to her."

"I'm worried about her, Dad?"

"Who, Jenny or Mrs. Wilson?"

"Jenny. It seems she doesn't even want to try to learn to walk again."

"I know. I've been spending a lot of time trying to figure out why not. Seems like she doesn't care if she ever gets out of that wheelchair. Any idea why that might be?"

"I don't know. . .maybe it's because . . ."

"Because? Because what, Patty?"

"I don't know, maybe it's because she just wants to stay down here. I mean, maybe she thinks as long as she can't walk and has to go to therapy, then we can't go back. Does that make sense?"

"Hmmm. I hadn't thought of it that way, but I suppose that could be it. You'd think she'd want to get back so she can go to school and see her friends. Do you know any reason she wouldn't want to go back home? I mean, I'm glad she wants to stay, and you know you're welcome to stay as long as you like, but Jenny's not walking is a pretty big price to pay."

"I know, Dad. I don't know what I'm going to do. I can't just stay here indefinitely. . .with no job. . .no life. . .and Jenny needs to get back in school. But I'm never going back to . . ."

"Back to? Back to what?"

"I'm never going back to *him*. But I don't want to talk about that right now."

"I understand, Patty...I think...but we need to talk about what might be preventing Jenny from even trying to walk again. Don't you agree?"

Patty sat for a long time, staring off into the valley. Eventually, she said, "Maybe she's afraid to go back. . .afraid he might . . ."

"Afraid he might what, Patty? Did that bastard do something to Jenny?"

"I—I don't know. Maybe. She said he . . ."

"She said he *what*?"

"She just said some things. . .things I can't believe. But I don't want to think she's making them up, either. So just in case she's not, I don't ever intend to be in a position where he can get near her again. Maybe that's why she. . .Oh, Daddy, I've screwed up my life so bad, and now maybe Jenny's, too. I feel so awful. How can I be so stupid?"

"We'll work this out, Patty. It can't be as bad as you say."

"I'm afraid it could. If what Jenny says is true . . ."

"Oh, you know how kids exaggerate, Patty."

"Jenny doesn't usually say things that aren't true."

"What kind of things?"

"Just things. . .you know, like about how he . . ."

"How he. . .how he *what*?

"Well, just about him touching her, stuff like that. I still can't believe he'd do that, but—"

"That son-of-a-bitch! I knew there was something about him I didn't like. Patty, how could you—"

"Now, Dad! Don't get all worked up. Kirby's not such a bad guy. . .except sometimes when he's been drinking. You think I would've stayed with him so long if he was, you know, like *that*?"

"No, I guess not. . .but I agree you can't chance anything like that ever happening again. Any chance the bastard might show up here? In a way, I sort of wish he would. I'd like to—"

"No, Dad, he doesn't even know where I am. He doesn't know where you live, either. And if he did show up, I could maybe get him arrested, so I don't ever expect to hear from him again. . .which is perfectly okay by me. I've screwed everything up. What am I going to do?"

"You and Jenny should just plan to stay here, Patty. You can make a life here, you know. And Jenny can go to school here. This isn't such a bad place to raise a daughter, you know."

"I know, but I have to have a job. I can't just go on letting you pay for everything. And I need to have my own life. I mean, I don't even know anyone here, and there's nothing for me to do."

"You could teach."

"What? What'd you mean?"

"You've always wanted teach, right?"

"Yes, but . . ."

"You might get a job teaching at the high school down in Roan Creek. I hear they have a hard time finding math and science teachers. You were always good in those subjects."

"But I don't even have a teaching certificate. I'd have to go back to college and take—I don't know, probably several courses. . .and then do student teaching. That'd take months—maybe years."

"Well, maybe not. I have a friend—well, actually an old acquaintance. Her name is Sarah and she teaches at the high school. She was a year behind me in school here. I ran into her in the supermarket the other day and she told me she teaches science. She said they're so short of math and science teachers that they sometimes allow someone with a degree in those subjects to teach under a provisional certificate while they take the necessary courses. I think as long as you're working toward your certificate they'll let you teach. Might be worth checking into."

Patty smiled. "A lady friend, huh? Dad! That—that's—"

"Patty I hope you don't think—I mean, I'll always love your mother, you know that. . .don't you? But it's been over three years and . . ."

"Yes, of course. And you don't need to feel. . .well, I know you need someone, Dad. You can't be expected to live alone forever. I mean, who am I to be giving you advice about this sort of thing? But Dad, it's okay with me if you meet someone. . .I mean somebody special. Is this lady, I mean . . ."

"I don't know, Patty. To be honest, I guess I have to admit that there's a possibility. . .but it's too soon to know. Sarah lost her husband a few years ago, so we have that in common. But right now, we're just friends. I don't know if it'll ever develop beyond that. However, I appreciate knowing that if it did, that would be okay with you. I worry about these things, you know. Anyway, what do you think about this teaching idea?"

"I don't know, Dad. . .maybe. But I don't think I'm quite ready for that just yet. Maybe when Jenny. . .Oh, Dad, what if she never walks again? How will I ever be able to live with myself?"

"She'll walk again, Patty. Maybe she just needs to know that. . .well, maybe when things become a little more stable—I mean in your life. . .you know, when you decide what you're going to do. If you should decide to stay here, maybe that would somehow help Jenny to. . .it's just something to think about. I'm not trying to tell you what to do."

"I know. Thanks, Dad. I just need some time to sort things out."

"Okay, that's fair. If you decide you want to check into this teaching possibility, just let me know and I'll talk to Sarah and ask her to. . .well, she could probably get you an appointment with the principal, or whoever you need to talk to about it."

"Okay, maybe in a few days. Right now, though, I better start supper. Jenny'll be waking up soon. How's fried chicken sound for tonight?"

"Sounds great."

"Dad."

"Yes."

"Thanks for being here for me."

"You know I always will be."

"I know. I love you, Dad."

For the first time in a long time, Patty came over, put her arms around me and we hugged for a long time, as each of us tried to hide the tears forming in our eyes.

Chapter 15

I loaned Patty enough money so that when added to the insurance settlement amount, she had enough to purchase a new Dodge Caravan. This one was white and had four captain's chairs plus a bench seat across the back that could be removed in order to fit Jenny's wheelchair. Jenny seemed almost indifferent about the new car, but showed no fear of riding in it, as we had anticipated she might.

A few other notes had appeared in the mailbox. I usually read only portions of them to Jenny, sometimes changing the words so they made more sense and leaving out things that Patty and I didn't feel were appropriate for Jenny to hear. It seemed the old lady was simply missing Jenny and wanting to see her. Jenny kept asking when she was going to get to see Clara again, so finally I talked with Patty about inviting the old lady over to spend some supervised time with Jenny. Patty reluctantly agreed and we decided we would invite her over for dinner soon.

The morning was warm and sunny with hardly any wind. Jenny and kitty were sitting out on the front porch, while Patty puttered around in the kitchen preparing lunch.

Jenny was working diligently on a picture of Garfield in the new coloring book her mommy had bought her yesterday after the doctor's appointment.

The coloring book lay across a board that spanned the arms of the wheelchair. Several crayons lay on either side of the book. Kitty was in her usual position, curled up in Jenny's lap. Jenny could hear her purring softly and imagined she was napping, as she usually did when outside in the sun.

Sparrows, robins and bluebirds skittered about in the yard, pecking in the grass. As one of the sparrows ventured near the sidewalk, Kitty's eyes darted back and forth, following the bird's every movement. Not only was the kitten wide-awake, but she was also alert and calculating. Every few seconds the tip of the kitten's tail flicked ever so slightly in response to the bird's movements. As the sparrow ventured ever closer to the edge of the sidewalk just beyond the porch, the kitten's tail began moving rhythmically in a strangely hypnotic manner, instinctively luring its prey into false comfort.

Suddenly the kitten leapt from Jenny's lap, landing on the sidewalk in an attack crouch. Then in a single bound it pounced on the exact spot where the bird had last been feeding, landing on all fours and grasping the air with its front paws, its small claws extended. The bird was no longer there, however, having taken flight upon the kitten's initial leap onto the sidewalk. Kitty looked around in surprise and noticed the bird flying low to the ground, heading across the yard in the general direction of the house under construction next door. Immediately, the kitten sprang forward and commenced chase, although of course it was no match for a bird in flight.

Upon the kitten's leap from her lap, Jenny flung the coloring book to the floor, scattering crayons across the porch. She grabbed the wheels of her chair, spun it around and moved closer to the edge of the porch.

"Amanda, you come back here! Bad kitty!"

When the kitten began chasing the bird across the yard, Jenny gasped, "Amanda, no! Come back."

Jenny threw the board onto the porch, wheeled her chair around and headed for the ramp. The chair picked up speed going down the ramp and rolled to a stop near the middle of the driveway. Glancing to her right, Jenny saw kitty bounding across the open space between Ole Pa's yard and that new house being built next door. She didn't know what the kitten was chasing, but guessed it might be a bird or a mouse.

Grasping the wheels of her chair, Jenny pushed with all her might, propelling herself across the driveway and into the yard. Her arms soon began to ache as she struggled to keep the chair moving through the soft grass. She had to find Amanda or the kitten might get lost and never be found. With determination, she pushed harder. Still with several yards to go, her muscles began to ache to the point she felt she couldn't go any farther. But she wouldn't quit. She became more and more angry with herself for her inability just to jump out of this chair and run across the yard.

Why couldn't she do it? Maybe if she just stood and tried to walk, she would be able to do it. But then something convinced her that she would fall flat of her face if she tried, so she just stopped and sat for a few moments, trying to decide what to do. Then she started pushing the wheels again, struggling with all her might to make them roll slowly through the grass. Finally, with one mighty surge, she propelled the chair onto the edge of the gravel driveway leading to the new house. This slowed her progress even more now, as the wheels crunched into the small pieces of crushed rock. Forcing her aching arms to keep pumping, she slowly made her way up the driveway toward the garage, which was framed but as yet had no door enclosing it.

As Jenny neared the entrance, she stopped and listened. Hearing nothing, she called out, "Amanda. . .Amanda."

Cocking her ear, she thought she heard a soft mewing originating from somewhere inside the house. With determination, she propelled the chair up and over the lip of concrete forming the garage floor, which was covered with pieces of board and other scraps of building material. Weaving the little chair around the debris, she made her way toward the back of the garage. Once more, she stopped, called kitty's name and listened. A definite meow emanated from the direction of the interior door leading into the house. Jenny could see through the two-by-four studs framing the walls, but she didn't see kitty anywhere.

Again, she called, "Amanda! You come out here, right this minute. You're in big trouble, kitten!"

Clara Wilson had promised to take Omega for a long walk this morning. He had kept her warm last night and she owed it to him, although she knew, of course, why he wanted to go. He was anxious to see those bitches that lived in the house down near the highway. Probably one of them was in heat. Well, she would take him for a walk as promised, but if he tried to mess around with either of those dogs, she would be mighty upset. She might even have to give him a spanking.

"Bad doggie! I know what you're thinking," she warned as she stroked Omega's head. His ears lay back flat and he whimpered softly. "Okay, I'm gonna take you out for a walk, but you gotta promise not to go running off after either of them she devils. You promise? Huh, big fellow? Promise mommy you'll be good."

The big Lab jumped up and began licking Clara's face. "Okay, you promised, so you better behave. Come on now, let's go."

Clara had to fight back several of her other dogs to keep them from getting out as she opened the front gate for her and Omega. Maybe Jenny would be out on the porch this morning, she considered, as she headed down the road toward Carter's house. The weather was nice and the little girl often sat out on the porch in the mornings when it was warm enough. Too bad that woman who claimed to be Jenny's mother had warned Clara to stay away. Clara knew that Jenny liked her and wanted her to be her mother instead of that blond woman. It wasn't fair she got to have Jenny all to herself. Soon Clara would have to figure out some way to change things. After all, Jenny was supposed to be hers.

The little girl wasn't out on the porch as Clara had hoped, so she and Omega made their way on down the road toward the highway. As they passed the driveway leading to the new house under construction, Omega suddenly stopped. His ears perked up, he cocked his head in the direction of the house and began whimpering.

"What is it, boy?"

Clara was aware that sometimes the dogs from down the street strayed up in this direction. Maybe Omega had sensed one of them somewhere over near that new house. He was looking in that direction, whining, his tail wagging vigorously. Every so often, he looked up at Clara as if to say, *come on, let's go.*

Suddenly the big dog bolted. He ran at a full gallop down the driveway toward the partially constructed house. Clara cursed under her breath. Now she would have to go chasing after him.

"Omega, you come back here," she yelled, but to no avail, as the big dog disappeared into the garage.

Hearing the dog barking now, Clara hurried up the driveway as fast as her old legs would carry her. Omega was being a bad boy and he would have to have a spanking for sure. She couldn't allow him to behave this way. He was as bad as her dead husband used to be about chasing after other women.

Patty had just put lunch on the table. She walked out to the front porch to bring Jenny inside to eat. Opening the front door, she stepped out onto the porch and said, "Sweetheart, time for..." She looked around, panic overcoming her. "Jenny? Jenny! Where are you? Oh, God!"

She turned back toward the door. "Dad! Dad! Come quick!"

"What—what's going on?"

"She's gone! Jenny's gone!"

"What—where? Have you looked around the side of the house? Maybe she—"

"Not yet. You go that way and I'll go this way. We'll meet in the back."

Patty ran across the driveway and around the house on that side while I headed in the other direction. We met at the back door. Patty looked around wildly and I then noticed her gaze freeze on the boulder near the edge of the bluff directly behind the house.

"No, Patty. I'm sure she wouldn't have gone near the edge. We've talked to her about that too many times."

"Unless. . .what if that kitten ran back there, chasing some bird or something. Maybe Jenny went after it and her chair—oh, God, Daddy, what if . . ."

Patty bolted for the edge of the cliff and I followed. We stood on the edge of the large boulder, scanning the area underneath, but couldn't see any sign of Jenny. Patty called her name several times and we listened. Nothing.

"She took her! I just know it! That old lady took her," Patty shouted. "Who knows what she's doing with my baby? Daddy, we gotta do something!"

"Patty, I don't think Clara would—"

"Yes, she would! She's got Jenny! I just know it!"

Patty turned and ran back toward the house. "Come on, Dad, we've got to find her." She continued around the side of the house, heading toward the Wilson place. "Dad! Come on! I know she's over there!"

I caught up with Patty as she reached the edge of the yard and we ran down the road in front of the Wilson property. Several dogs began barking simultaneously, jumping and scratching at the fence facing the road as we reached the front gate.

"Patty, we can't go into that yard. They'll attack us."

"Then what are we going to do? I know she's got her inside. Who knows what she's up to? We have to call nine-one-one—or the sheriff, or something!"

Glancing toward the house next door, I noticed Mrs. Peterson outside in her yard, leaning on a rake, watching. I had frequently seen Mrs. Peterson out working in her yard when the weather was nice. She had stopped what she was doing and appeared to be watching and listening, trying to figure out what was going on. I headed in her direction and Patty followed.

"Morning, Mrs. Peterson. Have you seen my granddaughter, Jenny—the little girl in the wheelchair? She seems to have disappeared."

Before the lady could answer, Patty added, "Did you see that old lady take her inside? Did you see her pushing a little girl in a wheelchair?"

"No, sorry. I haven't seen the little girl. I've been working out here for about an hour, so I probably would've seen her if she'd come this way. How long has she been missing?"

"We don't know," Patty replied. "She was sitting out on the porch playing and I went out to get her for lunch and she was gone. I know this crazy old woman took her! Have you seen the old lady out and about this morning?"

"Well, yes, as a matter of fact I did. She left just a few minutes ago, with that big black dog of hers that she takes nearly everywhere with her now. I think she headed down the road toward the highway."

"That's it! I knew it!" yelled Patty. "She's taken Jenny and headed down toward that highway. She might push her right out into road—come on, Dad, let's go!"

Hearing another meow from somewhere inside the house, Jenny grasped the wheels of her chair and pushed herself closer, picking up speed as the wheelchair rolled across the smooth concrete floor. She didn't see the piece of two-by-six board until her right wheel struck it, causing that side of the chair to come to a sudden stop. The other wheel kept rolling, jerking the wheelchair sharply to the right. Jenny's momentum carried her forward, flinging her out of the chair. Instinctively, she turned sideways and stuck out her left arm to break her fall. Her left elbow struck the concrete floor sharply, sending excruciating pain up her arm. She screamed, and then as her body sprawled onto the concrete floor in a heap, she began sobbing.

When the old woman finally made it to the garage and looked inside, she gasped. Omega was hovering over the little girl, who lay on the garage floor beside her wheelchair. Both the dog and the girl were whimpering as Omega licked the little girl's face. Occasionally, the dog would stop licking and look at Clara as if asking her to help.

Clara hurried across the garage to Jenny. "Oh! Child, what happened? Are you all right?" Jenny continued to sob as Clara knelt beside her, lifted her head and placed it in her lap.

The old lady then tried to lift the little girl back into her wheelchair, but after struggling for a minute, she found that she couldn't do it. She then lay Jenny back down, resting her head in her lap. Omega continued to lick tears from the little girl's face.

Clara had to do something, but she wouldn't leave Jenny alone on the floor crying while she went for help, so she commenced yelling, "Help! Somebody, help." Surely, someone over at the Carter house would hear her. Didn't they even know Jenny was missing? Clara wouldn't be surprised if they didn't, since they didn't care about the little girl the way Clara did. If Jenny lived at her house like she was supposed to do, Clara would take care of her.

Jenny continued to sob as Clara stroked her head. From time to time, she again yelled for help, but it seemed no one was coming. She tired to think of something else to do, but she refused to leave the little girl alone, so all she could think to do was continue yelling for help.

Patty sprinted down the road and I followed as fast as he could. By the time she passed in front of our house, I was several yards behind. Halfway between my mailbox and the driveway to the new house next door, Patty suddenly stopped. Turning toward the house, she cocked her head, listening.

When I caught up with her, she said, "Dad, listen. Did you hear someone yelling?"

We stood for a moment, listening. Then it came again, the unmistakable sound of a woman yelling. It seemed to be coming from the direction of the new house.

Patty raced down the driveway. I following as fast as I could. When she reached the entrance to the garage, she stopped suddenly. Her hand flew to her mouth. By the time I reached the garage entrance, Patty had disappeared inside. I looked inside and saw her kneeling beside Jenny, who lay sprawled on the concrete floor beside her wheelchair. The little girl's head was in Clara Wilson's lap and the big black dog was licking Jenny's face. I watched as Patty jerked her daughter away from the old lady and then slapped and yelled at the dog, chasing it back a few paces.

"Baby, are you okay? What did this crazy old woman do to you?"

Jenny's crying increased in intensity and she flung her arms around her mother's neck and clung to her. Patty turned toward the old woman. I had never seen my daughter look so angry.

"You crazy old—why did you do this? You crazy old witch! I told you to stay away from her! Now look what you've done."

The old woman backed away, tears streaming down her face.

I said, "Patty, I'm sure she didn't—"

"Yes, she did! She did this to Jenny! That's why I didn't want her around. That crazy old woman's hurt Jenny and she's going to pay for this." Patty glared in the direction of the old woman, who had by now turned and was walking slowly out of the garage, Omega sidling along beside her

"That's right! Get out of here! I don't ever want you near Jenny again," Patty yelled. "I warned you to stay away from her. If she's hurt, I'm calling the sheriff. I'm gonna have you arrested!"

The old woman continued out the driveway, her shoulders jerking with sobs. I didn't know what he should do. It seemed the old woman had pushed Jenny over here and somehow allowed her to fall out of her wheelchair. I was certain it had been an accident, though, and didn't think we needed to get the sheriff involved. Still, somehow we had to keep the old lady away from Jenny. But I would handle that later. Right now, we needed to get Jenny back into her wheelchair and take care of her injuries.

"Dad, help me get her into the wheelchair," Patty yelled.

We gently lifted the little girl into her wheelchair. Jenny was still sobbing, but between sobs she was trying to tell us something. "Kitty. . .she ran away. . .I was chasing her. Clara didn't. .

.she didn't do anything. . .she found me after I fell. . .she was just trying to help."

I heard a *meow* and noticed the kitten appear in the doorway leading from the house into the garage. The kitten then jumped down, came running over and leapt into Jenny's lap.

"Bad kitty!" Jenny said. Then she looked up and said, "Mommy, you. . .you shouldn't have said those mean things. . .Clara didn't hurt me. . .she was just trying to help."

Patty put her hand over her mouth and gasped. Then she turned, ran out of the garage and caught up with Clara just as she reached the road. "Clara, I—I'm so sorry. I thought. . .I'm so sorry." She placed her hand on the old woman's arm, but Clara jerked away and kept walking.

"Get away. . .mean woman. . .leave me alone."

"Clara—Mrs. Wilson, I'm so sorry. I thought that you. . .I'm so sorry. Please forgive me."

Clara Wilson continued out into the road, turned and headed toward her house.

Patty followed, pleading, "Please, Mrs. Wilson, I'm so sorry. I know you were trying to help Jenny. I'm sorry I said—"

"Mean woman. . .don't deserve to have her," Clara mumbled. "Think I'm crazy, just like all the rest." She then turned and glared at Patty. "Well, you're the crazy one! Get away from me. Leave me alone!"

Clara then picked up her pace and finally Patty gave up. She turned and walked back toward Jenny. Patty looked back over her shoulder and watched the old woman disappearing into her yard. She felt just awful.

Turning to Jenny, Patty said, "Sweetheart, I'm sorry. Are you okay?"

"My elbow hurts. . .but I guess I'm okay. Clara was just trying to help me, Mommy. You didn't need to be so mean to her."

"I know, sweetheart. I'm so sorry."

Jenny looked down at the kitten and said, "Bad kitty! You know you're in big trouble."

Clara Wilson stumbled into her house and headed directly into her bedroom where she fell across her bed. A mournful wail filled the room. She lay there for several minutes, her body racking with sobs. The big dog crawled up onto the bed beside her and she turned onto her side, wrapping her arms around him. Omega then began licking her tears away.

After a few minutes, Clara's sobbing subsided and she felt her eyelids drooping. This time she didn't even try to prevent her eyes from closing, and before long she felt herself slipping into a blissful slumber. Her last conscious thought was that she no longer cared whether she ever woke up.

Clara was flying, floating gently downward like a hang-glider taking advantage of the trailing edge of a dying updraft. She looked to her right and there he was, gliding along beside her. It was Gordy—a young Gordy in all his glory. She imagined he was smiling at her. Glancing to her left, she saw Omega, also floating along beside her.

Suddenly she began picking up speed. The ground was fast approaching. She looked around and noticed that Gordy had disappeared, but Omega continued to fall with her. Faster. Faster. The ground rushed up to meet them.

"Noooo!"

Clara wasn't conscious of hitting the ground, but then suddenly she was swooping upward again, as if she had bounced, like on a trampoline. Looking down toward the ground, she saw Omega lying there in a broken heap. She could see and feel his pain as he rolled his eyes upward. She knew he was dying. At the same time, she realized that she was already dead; yet, it seemed that she wasn't.

Looking down again, she noticed the body of an old lady lying near the big black Lab. Clara watched as the dog struggled across the old woman's body and began licking her face. Floating upward then, Clara glanced to her right and noticed Gordy was with her again. He smiled at her, his tongue wagging and his ears extended forward, just as they always did when he was happy or excited.

Glancing downward now, Clara saw Omega leave the ground and begin rising toward her. Moments later, he took his place alongside and she and her two faithful companions floated upward into the clouds.

Clara awoke suddenly to find Omega licking her face and whimpering. She hugged the big dog and then struggled to her feet and stumbled into the bathroom. Soon it would be time to go, she thought, as she washed her face. Yes, very soon. Maybe tomorrow. . .or it could even be tonight. But she was ready—well, almost ready. First, she had to do one more thing.

Taking a piece of paper and a pen from the drawer of her bedside table, Clara began scribbling a message. She had to let the little girl know that she was leaving and what to do after she was gone. Clara had to make sure Jenny understood about the angels. . .and about the tree.

Chapter 16

For the past several days, I had been taking a morning walk. Afterwards, I sometimes sat out on a big rock near the bluff behind my house, staring off into the valley and allowing my mind to wander. Mostly I thought about Jenny, wondering why she refused even to try to learn to walk again. Weeks had passed since the accident and the doctors could find no physical reason preventing her from walking. Strangely, she remained enthusiastic about her physical therapy, and more than anything, she seemed to look forward to spending time with Tony. Still, for some reason this didn't seem to be helping.

I thought a lot about what Patty had said about why Jenny might not want to go back home. I wondered if at the subconscious level Jenny refused to allow herself to get better because she was afraid that if she did she might have to go back to her previous life. If even a portion of what Patty had alluded to was true, then I could understand how this might possibly be the case.

I was aware that my daughter still blamed herself for the accident. Probably I would feel the same way were I in her position. At least she had finally agreed to meet with officials at the high school to discuss a possible teaching position. I had called his friend, Sarah, who had arranged an appointment for Patty to meet with the assistant principal the following week.

The bizarre idea had come to me in phases, a glimmer jutting into my consciousness for a brief instant, only to disappear and then resurface when least expected. I tried to force the concept from my mind, but it kept returning, nagging at me, frequently in the middle of the night when I couldn't sleep, which was becoming more of a problem lately.

So many years had passed since those seemingly miraculous events had occurred in my childhood, and I wasn't even certain now that they had ever actually happened. Yet, as the days passed, the idea persisted until it was becoming almost an obsession. I realized I should talk with Patty about this first; but if I did, she would no doubt conclude that I had strayed over the edge, joining Clara Wilson in her *never-never land*. Which might well be the case, I realized. Patty would likely negate the whole thing, and perhaps she would be right. This probably *was* a foolish notion. Still, I couldn't stop thinking about it as I sat on my favorite rock on the edge of the bluff this morning looking off into the valley.

After a while, I began to reflect on my growing-up days down there. Allowing my mind to travel back to the time when I first discovered the magic, I could clearly remember that day when I'd confirmed that there was indeed something special about that tree...

From the first time I noticed the tree, when I was about seven years old, I had felt drawn to it. All the trees in the park across the street from my house were huge, extending hundreds of feet into the air, as measured in the mind of a young boy.

When I first saw those giant trees, I marveled, having never seen trees so tall as these. My father told me that most of them were maple trees, and I soon learned that my special tree was actually a *sugar* maple. I didn't know why I thought of this particular tree as special. It might have been slightly taller than the other trees, but I could have been imagining that. The tree not only seemed taller than the other trees around it, but also fuller and more alive. In the summer when the afternoon sun was just right, the shadow of this tree fell completely across my house, which was on the other side of the street from the tree.

During the first few months I lived across from this tree, I set out to learn as much about it as I could. I quickly discovered the special aroma it gave off and the sound of the wind whistling through its branches. Often I rubbed my hands across the rough, scaly bark, memorizing its feel. In class at school when bored, I drew pictures of the leaves, sometimes sketching single leaves and other times drawing the pattern made by several leaves on a branch. I had noticed that the toothed leaves grew in pairs, one from each side of its small branch, and nearly all the leaves had five points, although some had only three, and a few had as many as seven.

Sometime during that first year, I began to consider the possibility of someday climbing this tree. Frequently I stood underneath the branch nearest to the ground and jumped as high as I could, but was never able to come even close to touching it. Other branches grew farther up the tree from that lowest branch, extending out in various directions, two-to-three feet apart. If I could just find some way to get onto that lowest branch, then I could easily climb to the top of the tree. This was not to be, however, because I could never think of any way to reach that first branch. Not that I would admit it at the time, but the real reason I didn't come up with a way to reach the branch was that I would have been too scared to climb the huge tree, even then. The only trees I had ever climbed were the small saplings growing in our backyard, but they were only about ten feet tall, and I only ever got about five feet off the ground, just high enough for the tree to bend, and as I pushed out with me feet and held on, the tree would give me a gently ride to the ground.

Nearly every day I played around the base of the huge sugar maple, sometimes making roads in the dirt around its roots for my toy trucks and cars to travel. I kept looking up at that lowest branch, which was about as big around as my waist, wondering how I might ever be able to reach it. By then, I had made up my mind that someday I would find a way to climb this tree.

As the weeks and months passed, I continued to explore the tree. One day I thought of a way to measure its diameter. I took a fishing line and stretched it around the trunk of the tree. Then I laid the line out straight on the ground and measured it with a yard stick, determining that the tree was fifteen feet and nine inches around. I thought this was large for a sugar maple, because I had by now looked up the characteristics of this type tree in the school library.

During the first autumn after discovering the tree, I watched in wonderment as its leaves changed from dark green to brilliant yellow, then orange, and finally red, creating the most splendid sight I had ever seen. The tree seemed to feel some sort of pride in its own beauty, reminding me of a peacock I had seen at the zoo last summer. I had watched as the pretty bird spread its tail feathers, fanning them out like a rainbow and then strutting about, as if proud of its loveliness. This tree seemed to feel pride in this same way.

One day I noticed the leaves were beginning to fall from the trees, and I felt sad watching the dead leaves float to the ground. Collecting some, I kept them in a box underneath my bed. Sometimes in bed late at night I would put my hand underneath the bed and feel the leaves with my fingers. Just touching them made me feel good.

In the springtime, when small buds began to emerge, I rejoiced along with the tree as it came alive again. My father had explained that the winds took some of these seeds high into the air and they drifted to many other areas to create new trees. Although I searched for baby trees, I never found any coming up.

It was in the summer of my eighth year when I first came up with the idea for a way to climb this tree. I got the idea from an episode of the *Leave it to Beaver* TV show, wherein Wally and some of his friends had decided to build a tree house. I watched in amazement as the boys nailed pieces of an old two-by-four to the tree trunk to make a ladder. Thinking this an ingenious way for me to be able to reach that lower branch, I wondered why I'd never before thought of doing this. I had so often stood underneath the tree, just looking up at that branch so far above; yet, never once had I been able to think of any way to reach it. Maybe it was because I was afraid I would have to admit that I hadn't really wanted to find a way to reach that lower branch— until now, that is. I was ready to climb his tree now, and knew it was ready for me.

Hardly able to wait until the next afternoon after school, I raced home, got my daddy's saw, and cut an old two-by-four into four pieces, each about two feet long. Then, taking several large nails and a hammer from a toolbox, I set out for the tree. First, I tried holding one of the boards against the tree trunk and driving a nail through the board into the tree, a feat that turned out to be much more difficult than it had at first seemed. Finally deciding to lay the board on the ground, I drove a nail through the board first, then held the board against the tree and began pounding the nail.

After the third stroke of the hammer, when I felt the nail bite solidly into the tree, I experienced an odd sensation. My hands began to tremble. Dropping the hammer, I stood staring at the tree. Suddenly the piece of two-by-four came loose from the tree and fell to the ground, striking me on the leg. Something was dreadfully wrong, although I couldn't imagine what it might be.

Tentatively, I touched the tree near where the nail had entered and somehow knew then that this tree could feel. Moreover, the tree seemed to be crying, its tears streaming out through the hole made by the nail. I guessed the tree must have felt the nail and had been hurt by it. But how could that be? Trees couldn't feel. And even if they could, how could I possibly know what this tree might be feeling? I stood staring at the syrupy liquid seeping out through the nail hole. After a few moments, I put my hand underneath the hole and allowed the sticky substance to drain out into my hand.

But I still had to climb this tree. That had been my goal for several weeks now, and I wasn't about to give up because of some stupid feelings, especially from a dumb old tree. Slowly, I picked up the board and hammer, placed the board against the tree, drew back the hammer and swung it toward the board as hard as I could. The hammer slammed into my thumb and I yelled loudly, dropped the hammer and ran around the tree screaming. Then I sat with my back against the tree, holding my thumb inside my other hand, tears streaming down my face. The awful pain nearly made me nauseated.

After a while, the pain eased some and I dared make another attempt to nail the boards onto the tree. This time when I swung the hammer back, it slipped from my hand and I heard it land in some tall grass several feet behind me. Again, I stood glaring at the tree. Noticing the sap that still oozed from the nail hole, I placed my fingers underneath the hole and again allowed the sticky liquid to spread onto my hand. Touching my fingers to my tongue, I was surprised at the sweet taste. I was also amazed at how this made me feel, just savoring the sweet taste and aroma.

But I still meant to nail those boards to the tree, because now I was even more determined to climb this tree today. After locating the hammer in the weeds, I returned to the tree and held the board against it, this time with my hand nowhere near the nail. I swung the hammer as hard as I could and it slammed into the board, landing more than two inches from the head of the nail. *Whinnnng!* The board split and the nail popped out, whizzing by my head like a bullet. I heard it hit in the weeds behind me. Then the pieces of board fell to the ground, one of them striking him on the leg again. Stepping back, I put my hands on my hips and glared at the tree.

After a while, I approached the tree again and touched it at the place where the nail had entered. As the liquid continued to drain slowly from the nail hole onto my hand, I began to feel warm all over, as if this were some sort of elixir that was somehow entering my body through my fingertips, like magic. As it traveled up my arm and throughout my body, every area it entered felt warm and wonderful. This tree was definitely trying to tell me something—perhaps that it had magic powers.

Then I began to feel stupid. Trees did *not* have magic powers. I glanced over my shoulder to see if anyone else was around. Finding myself alone in the field, I again picked up the hammer. Suddenly I felt the tree shudder. "Don't worry, I'm not going to hurt you," I heard myself explaining. Then I said to myself, "Yeah, I must be crazy, talking to a dumb old tree like this."

Then I noticed that the tree seemed to wilt, causing the tips of its lower branches to appear to move closer to the ground. Or was I imagining this? That's what it had to be, just my imagination. I discovered, however, that I could nearly touch the end of one branch now as it hung only a foot or two above my reach. Probably this must be because I had grown taller over the past few months.

Walking underneath the end of the lowest branch, I jumped as high as I could and grasped a handful of leaves, which immediately stripped off in my hand. The limb then sprang up, causing me to fall to the ground. The leaves I held in my hand felt alive, and again I sensed the tree's sadness. Looking up at the tree, I felt ashamed for having pulled off its leaves. Dropping the leaves, I got up, ran over to the tree and placed my hand against the trunk, hoping the tree might somehow sense my sorrow.

A few minutes later, I reluctantly left the tree and headed home. I needed to think about all that had happened. That night I had trouble falling asleep, feeling as if the tree had more to tell me. I wanted to get out of bed and sneak back out to the tree, but dared not at such a late hour.

The next morning, after hardly any sleep, I jumped out of bed and ran barefoot to the tree, feeling that I just had to touch it again. As soon as I approached the tree, I noticed something strange. Funny, I had never before noticed those sprouts growing out from the tree trunk at distances of about three feet and six feet above the ground. It seemed as if this tree was growing new branches.

Of course, they must have been there all along and I had simply never noticed. Surely they must have been, although I was nearly certain they had not. After all, I had been studying this tree for months, and would have noticed such a thing. Right now, though, I had to hurry home and get ready for school.

All day at school, I could think of nothing other than the tree, and when I finally returned home that afternoon, I immediately ran across the park toward the tree. Even before I got close, I noticed something even more remarkable. Surely I was just imagining it, but those new branches appeared somehow to have grown even longer since this morning. They now extended out more than a foot from the tree, and small green leaves were beginning to sprout from their ends. These branches were about an inch or so in diameter, much smaller than the other branches, but large enough for me to stand on to reach that lower main branch.

I couldn't wait any longer! Somehow, I sensed that this tree wanted me to climb it, right now. After all, why else would it have grown a ladder for me? As soon as I touched the lower of the two new branches, I felt the magic. I didn't know how I could pull myself up to where I could stand on this branch to be able to reach the next higher one, but suddenly I felt myself almost floating, as I propelled myself up onto the branch. Without thinking, I grasped the next higher of the two new branches and somehow easily pulled myself up onto it. From there, I was able to reach that large main branch that had for so long eluded me.

Almost afraid to reach up and touch the large limb, which was now only a few inches above me, I stood on the small branch for a few moments, considering how I had gotten up there so easily, and what I should do now that I was there. Tentatively reaching up, I grasped the large limb. My fingers felt the magic touch, and I felt as light as a feather. At the same time, I felt strength coming into my arms and legs. Without thinking, I pushed off the smaller branch with my feet, swung out from the tree and managed to get my leg up and over the main branch. Then with hardly any effort I pulled myself up onto it.

Standing erect now, I glanced down. Suddenly, this seemed much higher than it had looked from below. I had to be at least ten or twelve feet above the ground. This was the highest I had ever ventured, and the feeling was both frightening and exhilarating. Forcing myself not to look down again, I began climbing. Slowly and carefully I made my way up through the branches until, before long, I was high in the air. I could almost see over the top of my house.

Continuing to climb, I at last found myself in the highest part of the tree that I felt would support me. Never in my life had I imagined being so high above the ground, and never had I felt so free. From the treetop, the world looked amazingly different than I had ever imagined. I felt as if I were another person, just floating above the earth, maybe like an angel must feel looking down from above. Strangely, I was not at all afraid, as I soared above my world.

A gentle breeze caused the top of the tree to sway, and when I looked down now, I became a little dizzy, moving back and forth like the man I'd seen on the tall pole at the circus. Yet, I was still not afraid. Somehow, I knew this tree would hold me securely. Then slowly I began to realize something else. Somehow, I knew now how this tree might be able to help me. Although I didn't understand it, I began to feel that I need only believe strongly enough while up in the tree, and I would gain the power to make things happen. How I came to know this, I wasn't sure...I just knew it.

Over the years, the tree helped me a number of times—or at least I believed it did. With my newfound powers, or magic, or whatever it was the tree gave me, he seemed able to solve numerous problems: such things as how to deal with a class bully, and how to get the prettiest and most popular girl in class to notice me. These things just seemed easy when I got help from the magic tree. It seemed that all I had to do was climb the tree with a particular problem in mind and when I came down, I would somehow know the solution. Of course, one would ever believe this tree had anything at all to do with my success. And perhaps it didn't. I wasn't even sure I believed it myself. In any case, I decided never to tell anyone about my seemingly magic tree.

The last time I had climbed the tree was during my senior year in high school, only a few days before graduation. I had been trying to decide what he would do after graduation, and as soon as I came down from the tree, I suddenly knew the answer. Three weeks later, I joined the navy, having no doubt I would find some way to complete my education while in the service. Perhaps I might even decide to stay in for a career.

I never returned to the tree after that day. By the time came home on leave to visit my parents, they had moved to a new house across town, and for some reason I did not go back to the old neighborhood. Perhaps I was afraid to see the tree again, afraid I might learn that there was nothing magic about it after all. I realized even then that there was a good chance this had all been an illusion, something I had simply created in my mind. And if that were the case, I did not ever want to know for sure.

Chapter 17

Jenny had made kitty stay inside this morning. Amanda had been bad last time she was out, running away like that, and the kitty needed to be punished. The morning was a little cooler than normal, but the sun felt warm on the porch, out of the wind. Birds were singing and the dogwoods were beginning to bloom, their blossoms painting glorious white and pink splotches around the yard. Jenny noticed some red-breasted birds hopping around in the yard, probably Robins, she decided. Didn't that mean spring was nearly here?

Jenny didn't feel like playing with kitty today anyway, and she didn't feel like coloring either. "Read one of your new books," her mommy had said when Jenny complained about having nothing to do but sit outside in her wheelchair all day. Jenny didn't feel like reading either. What she really wanted to do was to get out of this stupid chair and run around and play, the way she used to do. She missed her friends, missed being able to run free, playing tag, hide-and-go-seek, and other fun things. Did they actually think she liked just sitting here in this chair, not being able to do anything without their help? How could they be so *stupid*?

Well, if they thought she liked it, then she guessed she had been doing a good enough acting job. Tony was the only with whom she dared let her guard down a little. He understood that she really did want to walk again, but that she just couldn't do it. Of course, he didn't know exactly why; none of them did. She had actually taken a couple of steps during her last therapy session, with Tony sort of holding her up. He had shrieked with excitement, "You doing soooo good, *mon*. You be walking again soon, Jenny."

Jenny knew now that she was *able* to walk—if only she could, that is. Something still prevented her from actually doing it. Deep down, she had a vague idea as to why she was not walking. She had even heard Ole Pa and Mommy discussing it one day when they thought she was asleep. Maybe they were right and it did have something to do with her not wanting to go back. Why would she not want to go back, they wondered? Naturally, she missed her friends and she missed school, but still, she was willing to give up all of that—even give up walking again—if it meant she never had to go back, never had to be near *him* again.

She knew that her mommy hadn't really believed her when she tried to tell her what *he* had done that night. She didn't understand how her mommy could have ever wanted to be around someone like *him*, anyway. He was a mean, awful man. Why couldn't Mommy see that? Jenny hated it most when he tried to make her call him *Daddy*. She hated *him*, and if she had to stay in this wheelchair for the rest of her life, she guessed she would just do it, if that meant never having to see *him* again. She hated her mommy, too, for staying with that awful man and for leaving her alone with him. Actually, she hated everybody—well, everybody except for Amanda. . .and Clara. . .and sometimes, Ole Pa. . .although he didn't understand either. No one did. How could they?

Having some idea of why she couldn't allow herself to walk again didn't make it any easier, of course. She did try to will her legs to move, to wiggle her toes like the doctor wanted, but *will* them as she might, she just couldn't seem to make them move. It seemed as if someone had turned off a switch inside her head, preventing the signals from reaching her muscles. And wasn't that sort of how the doctor had explained it? He said the shock to her spinal cord had caused the nerves to shut down, preventing brain signals from getting through to her leg muscles. Well, that sort of made sense; but the doctor didn't know everything. Nobody did. He had been saying for weeks that she should be healed by now, and he didn't understand why she couldn't walk yet. Jenny didn't even understand this herself, so how could she expect them to understand.

Her mommy had questioned her over and over when Jenny had tried to tell her what *he* had done that night while her mommy was gone. Jenny still had nightmares about it, dreaming that he was coming into her room again. She would awaken, sweating and trembling. She tried not to wake up Mommy or Ole Pa after her nightmares, but sometimes she couldn't help it. She never told them what she'd been dreaming about, though; just that she had a nightmare. Mommy would usually sit with her afterwards until she finally went to sleep again.

Jenny didn't have the dreams as much now as she had at first, though. Still, she was afraid *he* might just show up here one day and things would become just as they had been before. Her mommy would decide to go back with that awful man and he might do those horrible things to her again. But since he hadn't come after all this time, maybe he wasn't coming at all. She didn't think he had even called, although she couldn't be sure. Jenny hated her mommy when she thought about her wanting to spend time with *him*. How could she not know he was a bad, bad man?

Jenny closed her eyes and allowed the warm sunshine to bathe her face. Soon she began to feel drowsy and her head drooped. Maybe she would just rest for a while. In the background, she heard the birds chirping and singing in the trees surrounding the house. Somewhere down the road a dog barked. A gentle breeze was blowing, carrying with it a sweet fragrance of honeysuckle growing across the road.

Jenny thought of Clara and wished she could see her again. Maybe Clara would come over today. . .but no, Mommy had warned the poor old woman to stay away. Mommy had hurt Clara's feelings, so probably Clara would never come back. Jenny opened her eyes and glanced toward Clara's house, hoping she might see her, but she didn't. The dogs were all quiet over there this morning, too. Clara just needed a friend. She wasn't crazy like they said, and Jenny knew that Clara would never hurt her. How could *they* not know this?

Her eyes drifted closed again, drowsiness slowly overcoming her, until she reached a state of semi-awareness: half-asleep, yet half awake. She could still hear the birds singing, but perhaps they were singing in her dreams now. Deeper she sank. . .deeper . . .

Suddenly the little girl heard footsteps on the stairs. She cringed and slid farther down underneath the covers. Maybe if she pretended to be asleep, he wouldn't come in. The door opened slightly, a shaft of light from the hallway splaying across her bed. Then suddenly he was in the room. She didn't look up, but she could sense his presence.

"Please, God—please let him think I'm asleep. Make him leave me alone."

Of course, there was no God.

He sat on the edge of her bed. "Jenny, you asleep, little darling? Daddy came to tuck you in and tell you goodnight."

Her body stiffened. Maybe—just maybe—he did come only to say goodnight. But no, she somehow knew he was here for some other reason. He was going to hurt her, she just knew it. She didn't understand why he would want to hurt her, but she had sensed during dinner that something was different about him tonight. He acted strange and he had been drinking. She hated it when he drank. Why did Mommy have to go to that stupid baby shower tonight anyway? Jenny had been alone with him at other times, but never at night and with her mommy gone for such a long time.

She squeezed her eyes shut and clung to the sides of the bed. Through the covers, she felt his hand touch her shoulder.

"You're NOT my daddy!" she screamed. "Just leave me alone!"

She slid farther down into the bed and pulled the covers over her head.

"Sure I am, darling." His voice was gravely and mocking, the way he usually spoke when he had been drinking.

"Please, God, just make him go away and leave me alone."

She felt his hand moving along the covers, down across her body, stopping just above her waist. She bit her lip until she felt warm blood in her mouth. His hand slid down a little farther, his fingers moving across the covers. Her skin crawled.

"Daddy loves you. Don't you love Daddy?"

His hand moved farther down, and quickly she turned her back to him.

"Leave me alone! You're NOT my daddy! You're NOT!"

His hand slid a little farther down until it now rested on her buttocks. Slowly, he began moving his hand back and forth, pressing harder, his fingers squeezing. Then he began to move his hand slowly up and down her legs. She tried to scream, but no sound came forth. There was no one to hear her, anyway, and if she screamed he might hurt her worse.

Then she heard what sounded like a zipper opening and soon she felt a slow, rhythmic motion as the bed began rocking, slowly at first, and then faster. What was he doing with his other hand? She heard him moaning, gasping, his breath now coming in short bursts. Faster, his hand rubbed her harder, moving down between her legs, his fingers probing. Suddenly he moaned, and then with one final gasp, he squeezed her legs until tears flooded her eyes.

She wanted to scream, but there was no one to hear her.

Then he took his hand away. She could still hear his rapid breathing.

"Goodnight, little darling," he finally said. "No need telling your mommy about this. She won't believe you, you know. And if you tell, I may not be so nice next time."

She sensed him standing, heard his zipper closing. Maybe it was over. Maybe he would leave now. Maybe it had all been a bad dream.

Then she heard the bedroom door closing. She lay there sobbing for what seemed like hours, the covers pulled tightly over her head. She felt dirty, ashamed. But she hadn't done anything wrong. . .had she?

Maybe Mommy would come in when she came home and Jenny could tell her what he had done. She couldn't tell, though, even if her mommy did come in. She was afraid of what he had said about not being so nice next time. She cringed at the thought of what he had done and what he might do in the future.

"Jenny! Jenny! Sweetheart, are you okay? Were you having a bad dream?"

Jenny opened her eyes and realized she was sitting on the porch. She must have drifted off to sleep. She saw her mommy standing there, staring at her with a concerned look on her face.

"I—I'm okay, Mommy. I guess I just fell asleep. I was having a bad dream."

"You were making strange, whimpering noises. Are you sure you're okay?"

"I'm okay. I wanna go inside now. I want my kitty."

"Okay, sweetie. Lunch is about ready. And maybe after lunch we'll play a game, okay? How about a game of Monopoly? I bet we can get Ole Pa to play."

"Whatever."

What she really wanted was for them just to leave her alone. Of course, they wouldn't do that. They thought they had to pamper her, as if she were a baby. They acted as if they thought that since she was in a wheelchair, she must be retarded or something. They would never understand. Never! How could they? Clara understood. Why couldn't they be more like Clara? Instead, they had been mean to the poor old lady, and now Jenny might never see her again. She hated her mommy. She hated Ole Pa, too. She just wanted to be with kitty. Kitty was the only one who understood.

Chapter 18

I continued to think about the tree. Was there any chance it might help Jenny? Of course not, I concluded over and over. Naturally, I knew now that the magic had not come from the tree at all, but had originated in my own mind, convincing me that if I believed strongly enough, I could sometimes create or alter events. Even that, I wasn't so sure about. Maybe I had imagined the whole thing, and there had never been any magic of believing at all. Maybe everything just randomly happened to a person in life. On the other hand, sometimes I thought it all had a pattern, a purpose. Although I recognized the foolishness of such fantasies as believing a tree could create magic, as I had felt in my childhood, nothing else seemed to be doing Jenny any good. How could it hurt just to go have a look at the tree? I had always tried to teach my daughter and granddaughter that anyone could create their own magic, if only they believed strongly enough. And was this not the whole message of the tree, anyway? The tree did not create the magic. The magic came from within—from believing. Although believing in what, I wasn't so sure anymore. God? Nature? Miracles? I had witnessed all these in my life, but yet, I still wasn't sure how it all fit together. Maybe we were never meant to understand it all.

Although I knew I was acting like a foolish old man, something urged me onward. After all, if I didn't try, I would never know, and might always regret not having given the tree a chance. Perhaps the tree could somehow help Jenny believe that she could walk again, as it had once made me believe I could do all those things that were seemingly beyond my ability. Of course, Jenny wouldn't be able to climb the tree as I had so often done, and I certainly dared not attempt to climb the tree myself now, not at my age. Yet, maybe just touching the tree might convey some magic, some power, some hidden energy. What could it hurt to try?

Every day I turned the concept over in my mind, playing out possible scenarios, which were mostly negative. What if I couldn't even find the tree after all these years? Or what if I found it and nothing happened? Or worse, what if the tree had been cut down? Probably that would be the case, I concluded, so I should just forget about this foolish idea. Yet, alone at night when I couldn't sleep, the idea kept nagging at me. No amount of rationalization seemed to convince me what, if anything, I should do about it.

Having driven around the little town several times since moving back, for some reason I had avoided that particular street. Frequently, I thought about driving past my old house and looking across the street to see if my special tree was still there; yet, I had never been able to force myself to do so. I wasn't sure now that I should ever go back there. Either the tree would be gone, or I would find that there had never been anything special about it after all. Neither of these outcomes was acceptable to me, so I just avoided it. Obviously I was being a silly old man, yet something continued to prevent me from completely putting it out of my mind.

Some days later, I dropped Patty off at the hairdresser and then, as promised, took Jenny to McDonalds for a snack while we waited. Patty had an appointment to meet with the assistant principal at the high school the following day, and wanted to have her hair done first, so Jenny and I had some time to kill while waiting.

After we finished our Big Mac's, I looked at my watch and realized we still had probably an hour before Patty would be finished. As I helped Jenny into the car, I found myself contemplating actually driving past the site of my old house. It was only a few blocks away. And what was the big deal, anyway? Why was I so scared of going there again? I still couldn't decide if my greatest fear was that the tree would be gone, or that it would still be there and I would discover there was nothing special about it at all—never had been. Then all my illusions would be shattered.

Unable to make up my mind, I drove around town for a while, trying to decide what to do. Finally, Jenny asked, "Ole Pa. Where are we going?"

"Oh, uh...I just thought maybe I'd show you where I used to live when I was growing up here. Would you like to see where I played when I was a little boy about your age?"

"Sure, I guess so."

I was committed now—or perhaps should be. Again, I considered telling Jenny about the tree, and almost decided to tell her now, but then changed my mind. This was probably a huge mistake, and I didn't want Jenny to be disappointed if nothing came of it, which of course would be the case.

Slowly I drove through the little town. Then I circled the old courthouse and headed down the street past the newspaper office. Two blocks farther on, as I neared the turn onto my old street, a knot began to form in the pit of my stomach. My dread of what I might find, combined with the dread of what I might *not* find, intensified until I almost decided just to drive on past. I had come this close, though, what could it hurt just to drive by where I used to live?

Approaching the turn onto Elm Street, I noticed that the old house on the corner%I tried to remember who had lived there%had been replaced by a new brick, ranch-style house. I was happy to see that the rows of elm trees I remembered lining the street on either side were still there, although obviously much larger now. Perhaps my tree would still be there in the park too, exactly as I remembered it.

My heart pounded and my palms sweated as I turned onto the narrow street where I had lived when I was seven years old, when I had first come to know the tree. Again, I felt foolish as I proceeded slowly down the street. When I rounded the curve where the old house should have been, I was shocked to discover that the house was no longer there. Maybe I had taken a wrong turn, I rationalized, continuing on down the street. When I passed the next house beyond where my house had been, however, I knew it was true: my old house *was* gone.

Well, what had I expected? The house had been old, even when I had lived in it.

Driving on to the end of the street, I then turned into the driveway of the house on the corner. As I turned around, I tried to remember who had lived in this house. I had known nearly everyone in town back then and it bothered me now that I couldn't remember this family's name. Of course, what did it matter anyway? After turning around, I drove slowly past where I thought the old house should have been, fighting the urge to glance across the street to see if the tree might still be there.

Again, I wondered what I would do, even if the tree was still here. Maybe I would just take Jenny underneath it, sit for a while and see if I experienced any of those old feelings. Finally, I could stand it no longer—I had to know. Turning the car around, I again proceeded slowly down the street past where my old house had been. Turning my head slowly, I looked across the street into the park. My heart nearly stopped. I had to look again before I would believe what I was seeing: two lighted softball fields, some swing sets and a swimming pool, but no trees anymore. None. My heart nearly broke as my greatest fear became reality—my special tree *was* really gone. Oh well, at least now I could put this silly idea out of my mind once and for all.

"Ole Pa, can we stop at the swings? Please..." Jenny asked excitedly. "Is this where you used to play when you were a little boy?"

"No, Jenny...I mean, yes, this is where I lived, but those swings weren't here back when I lived here," I explained, my mind running in crazy circles.

"Would you push me in a swing? Pleeease!"

"I, uh. . .well, I want to drive around a little first. Maybe we'll come back here later, okay?"

Driving around town in a daze, I again he circled the courthouse, and as I passed the post office, I remembered how excited I'd been as a little boy when my father first allowed me to go to the post office alone for the first time. Continuing down the street, I tried to convince myself that I had perhaps taken a wrong turn earlier; maybe they had moved the street and I would find the tree after all. I knew, however, that this was not to be. As I again turned onto Elm Street and passed the site of my old house, I admitted that there was no mistake; the tree was definitely gone.

I stopped the car, got out and carried Jenny to the swings and began pushing her. She screamed with delight, demanding that I push her higher. My heart nearly broke, having to admit that this beautiful little girl might never walk again. Still, maybe all she needed was to believe strongly enough that she *could* walk. The tree might have helped her to believe that. . .well, it *might* have, had it still been there.

Chapter 19

Kirby left Knoxville at 8:15 in the morning, heading northeast on Interstate 40. It was another misty, dreary day, but this time Kirby's mood did not match the weather. He had awakened this morning in high spirits; before this day was over, he would find the woman and make her sorry she had ever messed with him. He might even beat up the old man too, just for the fun of it. And definitely, he would have a piece of that little girl's bottom for telling her mother all those lies about him. Yeah, a good spanking would be just the thing to set that kid straight. Yeah, that's what he would do. He would slap the woman around a little, then have his way with her, then slap her around some more. Maybe he would even make the kid watch. Just thinking about that excited him and he pressed the accelerator down harder, took another beer from the cooler on the seat beside him, downing it in two long swigs.

Kirby arrived in the outskirts of Asheville around midmorning. He didn't intend to spend much time driving around. If his plan worked, he would go directly to her old man's house. Since he had no idea on which side of Asheville the old man lived, he exited the freeway a few miles outside the city. Noticing a Denny's, he pulled into the parking lot, deciding that one of their notorious Grand Slam breakfasts might just hit the spot. Maybe he would get lucky and the waitress would be friendly—she might even be friendly enough to help him with his plan. If not, he had a backup plan.

Kirby's luck turned out even better than he could have imagined. Not only was the waitress sexy-looking and friendly, but he could tell she wanted him. By the time he finished his eggs and bacon, she had been back to his table three or four times, hovering over him, refilling his coffee cup, smiling that *come-on* smile and asking if there was anything more she could do for him. He knew exactly what she meant, and it had nothing to do with her serving him breakfast. According to her nametag, the girl's name was Rachel, and he made sure he called her by name several times; they usually liked that. He complimented her on what a great job she was doing, and long before his meal was over, he knew she would do it. She might even do it just as a favor, although he still planned to make it worth her while.

When she came to bring his check, Kirby began his spiel, already certain it would work. "Say, Rachel, I just wanna thank ya again and tell ya how much I enjoyed my meal. Your service with a smile—a damned pretty one too, I might add—made everything taste so much better. I'd like to put in a good word for you with your manager. Is he or she around?"

She blushed and said, "Well, thank ya. That's so nice of you to say. He's right up yonder at the cash register where ya pay. But ya don't have to do nothin' like that. I'm just happy to serve ya and if I've made your day a little brighter, why that's all the thanks I need."

She flashed those big blue eyes his way and then leaned a little farther over than necessary to place his check on the table, ensuring that one of her ample breasts brushed against his arm. Dammit! Too bad he was on another mission right now. Then it occurred to him that he would be passing this way again later in the day, so maybe he could stop here on the way back, assuming she might still be here. Hell, why not just ask her right now, he decided.

"Say, Rachel. I got some business over in Asheville, but I'm gonna be coming back this way later, probably around dinnertime. You still gonna be here then? Shore would make this ole Tennessee boy happy if he could see ya again later."

She smiled shyly and said, "Well, uh. . .I get off at five. But I guess I could wait for ya if you're not back here by then."

He knew it! This was more than he could have hoped for. It was going to be so easy now that he almost allowed himself to become concerned because it seemed too easy.

"That'd be mighty nice of ya, Rachel. Say, maybe you could help this ole boy out a little right now— with some information, I mean. I ain't been over in Asheville for a long time, see, and I'm trying to find an old army buddy of mine. All I got is his phone number, and I wanna surprise him—ya know, just show up at his place unexpected like. See what I mean?"

"Yeah, I guess so. But how could I he'p ya?"

"Well, I was thinkin', ya know, maybe you'd make a quick phone call for me, just to get the address, and then I could surprise him. I'd sure appreciate that—and I'd make it worth your while." Kirby took out a twenty-dollar bill and placed it conspicuously on the table, figuring that was more than she made here in two or three days. The look in her eyes confirmed his assumption. Hell, maybe ten dollars would have been enough.

"Why, I'd be happy to do that for ya. But ya don't have to pay me nothin'." She glanced back at the twenty-dollar bill.

"I insist, Rachel."

"Well, okay, thank ya. That shore would he'p to pay the rent. But whatever would I say so's they'd give me the address?"

"Well, I been thinkin' 'bout that, Rachel. I bet you're a good actress, right?—I can just tell from talkin' to ya. You're sure pretty enough. I bet that's what ya always wanted to be, right?"

"Well, yeah. . .how'd ya know?"

"Just the way ya handle yourself. Anyway, I don't wanna take too much of your time, so here's what ya can say. Listen carefully now. Just tell whoever answers that you're in the accounting department with the electric company—use whatever the name of your electric company is— you know what that is, don't you?"

She nodded and said, "Sure, it's Asheville Gas and Electric."

"Okay, say you're in the accounting department with Asheville Electric and that you're embarrassed to have to be calling, but you've had a problem with your computer and some of the mailing addresses have gotten mixed up between customers. Tell them some bills even got sent to the wrong addresses, and you want to fix the problem Then say, 'This is the Carter residence, right?' Got it so far, sweetheart?"

"Shore, that sounds easy enough, I guess."

"Okay, then give them a bogus address and say something like, 'Is that correct, Mr. Carter?' Of course if a woman answers, say 'Ms. Carter.' Got it?"

"I think so. I could say somethin' like, 'Y'all live at, uh, 1330 Jones Street' or somethin' like that, right?"

"You got it, honey babe. I knew you was smart. Then they'll prob'bly say *no*, and maybe they'll just give you the correct address right then and there without ya even askin'. If so, say thanks and hang up quickly. But if they don't, then go on and say somethin' like, 'Well, it's a good thing I called then, Mr.—or Ms.—Carter, or your bill might've gone to somebody else. Then we would've had a real hard time getting' it all straightened out. Could you please give me your correct mailin' address now, Mr.—or Ms.—Carter?' I think that'll work, but if they're still hesitant, just give them some sad story about how your boss is gonna be all over you if you don't get this all straightened out before the bills are due to be sent out. Tell them you got hundreds of other people to call. Got it?"

"Okay, I think I'n do that." She pronounced the word *that* as if it contained three syllables: *tha-yaa-te*. "I had the leadin' role in my senior class play. Ever'body said I done real good."

"Fine, Rachel. I bet ya did, too. Can ya take a minute and go make that call now?"

"Okay, I'll go do it while ya pay. Then I'll write the address down and give it to ya."

Kirby winked at her and flashed her his best smile. "Great. Thanks, darling. I hope I get to see ya on my way back tonight. You're a real sweetheart to do this for me. I owe ya."

"Nah, ya don't," she said, lowering her eyes and blushing. "I'm just proud t' he'p."

Kirby paid for the food and, as promised, he told the manager what a fine job Rachel was doing and that she deserved a raise. Kirby went on to tell the manager that he was just passing through, but that he came this way frequently on business trips and that he would stop here every time now, primarily because of Rachel's fine service.

As he was finishing his spiel, Kirby saw her approaching from the direction of the telephones. He couldn't tell by her expression whether she had been successful, and his pulse quickened as he considered that she might have screwed it all up and ruined it for him. If so, he would owe her, all right, but she wouldn't enjoy his paying of that debt.

He met her near the front entrance and relaxed somewhat when she smiled shyly and handed him a folded piece of paper. Kirby returned her smile, winked and whispered, "Thanks, Rachel; you're a sweetheart." He definitely owed her and decided he would indeed stop here on his way back so he could return her favor. Maybe she would be just as good at other things as she was at acting. In fact, he was certain of it, and could hardly wait to get back.

Chapter 20

Those eyes!

Patty sat, hypnotized, gazing into his deep, penetrating blue eyes. She felt as if she could almost see into his very soul—and he into hers, too. He was saying something. Vaguely, she heard some of the words as he began asking about her background. Although his eyes revealed a different message, she had to listen to what he was saying. Forcing herself to divert her stare, she began picking up on his words.

"Tell me a little about yourself, Ms. Carter. Like, where did you go to college? Your major. Any previous teaching experience. Things of that nature."

Patty sat across from the assistant principal at the high school. She had been amazed to discover how young he looked. Probably he was no older than she was, Patty surmised, as she involuntarily allowed her gaze to drop down to his hands resting on the top of his desk.

No ring on his finger.

She stared at the brass nameplate on the desk: *Paul Crowley*. A silly thought flashed through her mind that she wouldn't even have to change her last initial.

You idiot! You came here for a job interview. Now get hold of yourself!

Patty had been taken aback by the unexpected handsomeness of this man. The last thing she had expected was to have to interview with someone to whom she felt attracted. She had been nervous about the interview ever since she found out about it, but now the reason for that nervousness took on a whole new dimension.

Not married, huh?

This interview was definitely going to be more difficult even than she had imagined.

"I, uh. . .I graduated from the University of Tennessee. Math major. Oh, and I minored in Biology."

He smiled.

Oh, those eyes.

Patty forced herself to glance around the room. She noticed framed certificates on the walls, but she could hardly read them from where she sat. They looked like diplomas of some sort. She could see some large letters across the top of one certificate: North Carolina State. That was probably where he had gone to college.

"Hmmm. I guess there's no need asking if you like football, then," he was saying. "Think the Big Orange will win the national championship this year?"

"Uh, yes, I—I think they just might."

"I sure wouldn't bet against them."

Patty smiled demurely, then lowered her eyes and blurted without thinking, "Payton Manning's a big hero of mine—I mean, I. . .of course, I never met him, but . . ." She shook her head and felt her face flushing. "I'm sorry, I just—"

He chuckled. "Oh, that's all right. I know what you mean. Tell me why you want to teach, Ms. Carter."

Patty rambled on at some length about how this was what she had always wanted to do. She told him that she had done some substitute teaching years ago, but admitted that she had no experience in the job for which she was applying. Again, her eyes locked with his and she no longer knew exactly what she was saying as she swam in that vast sea of blue. Finally, she stopped speaking and realized he was speaking again.

"Well, we certainly need to fill a math teacher position, Ms. Carter. You can apply for a provisional teaching certificate, which can be good for up to three years. We do require, however, that you enroll in and complete the courses necessary for getting your official teaching certificate."

Patty only heard bits and pieces of what he was saying, but it seemed as if he might be offering her a job.

"We have a number of students who have trouble with math, so they're required to retake some courses in the summer if they want to be promoted. Perhaps you could start this summer. What'd you think, Ms. Carter? Wanna give it a shot?"

"I, uh. . .yes—yes I'd love to. Do I. . .uh, what do I do next? I mean—"

"I'll have my secretary provide you with the proper forms. There's not much to it, really—just the typical paperwork of this ever-increasing bureaucracy. I spend a great amount of my time pushing papers and most of the remainder dealing with the also increasing number of disciplinary cases that come my way. But I guess you'll learn all about that soon enough. Sure you know what you're getting into?"

Paul Crowley smiled and Patty noticed his gaze falling ever so subtlety down across the front of her blouse. She blushed, glad now that she had worn the blue blazer, and she involuntarily pulled it closed a little. There was no doubt that he noticed. His eyes dropped on down to his desktop where he pressed a button on the intercom and asked his secretary to step into the office. Patty allowed herself to breathe again.

"Mrs. Parker, would you please provide Ms. Carter here with the necessary forms to apply for an interim certificate. I think she's going to be joining our teaching staff soon."

"Yes sir, I'll go round them up." The lady looked at Patty, smiled and added, "You can stop by my desk on your way out, Ms. Carter."

Mrs. Parker turned and walked out of the office and Patty felt her heart beating faster. She hoped that Paul Crowley didn't notice; yet, how could he not? She was making a fool of herself, jeopardizing an opportunity to begin doing exactly what she had always wanted to do.

"Mrs. Parker can also give you the information you'll need about the required courses for a teaching certificate. There's not that much to it, really. Most members of our teaching staff take their required courses at the NC State branch down in Asheville.

They have night classes, so I don't think you'll have too much difficulty. Where do you live, Ms. Carter?"

"Uh, right now I'm staying with my father—I mean, just until. . .well, we live out on Roan Mountain, right on the eastern brow."

"Oh, yes, I know the area well. Mom and Dad had a cabin out there when I was growing up—sort of a weekend place. They sold it right after I went away to NC State, and I've always regretted that. I love it out there. It's so peaceful."

"Yes, it is that. A little boring sometimes, though."

Oh, God, he might think I meant . . .

He nodded and chuckled. "Hey, maybe sometime you'll invite me out to meet your father," he said in a more lighthearted tone. "I've heard about him. He's an author, right? One of our teachers, Sarah Wallace, was telling me about him. I guess they went to school together. Anyway, maybe we might talk him into coming down and speaking to our Drama Department. Believe it or not, for a small-town school, we have quite a few aspiring writers."

"Oh, uh—yes, I'm sure he'd be, uh, delighted to do that," Patty mumbled.

"I wonder if my dad and your dad knew each other back in school. It was an even smaller school back then, so they probably did. Dad graduated in fifty-nine. When did your father graduate?"

"Uh, nineteen sixty, I think. They probably did know each other."

"I'll ask Dad if he remembers your father—Tom Carter, right?"

"Yes, right."

Paul Crowley continued to look at her and smile for what seemed a moment too long. Then after an awkward silence, he stood, walked around his desk and offered his hand. "Thanks for coming by, Ms. Carter. I hope to see you again soon."

What does that mean?

She took his hand and stood, feeling her knees go weak. "Thanks for seeing me. I—I enjoyed. . .I mean, I'm sure I'm going to enjoy teaching here."

Why was she making such a damned fool of herself? Of course, she knew the answer: it was his *eyes*—those damned mesmerizing blue eyes that she could delve into and never come out. And he knew it, too. Damn him!

Finally realizing that she was still holding his hand, she quickly released it, backed away a step and mumbled, "I—I guess I'd better go now. I'll just stop by and get those forms and. . .thank you for seeing me."

"It's been my pleasure, Ms. Carter. Thank you for coming by. I hope to. . .to see you again soon."

Those damned hypnotic, alluring, erotic blue eyes. Does he even know the effect he's having? Oh yes, he knows. Damn him! He knows exactly what he's doing.

He was speaking again. "I'll call and let you know when the summer session is to begin, and what you need to do to get prepared." Smiling knowingly, he added, "Would you give me your phone number?"

Patty told him the number and he repeated it silently a couple of times, but he didn't write it down.

Then without saying anything, he took a business card from a holder on his desk and handed it to her. She glanced at it briefly, then put it in her purse.

"Usually the teachers come in a week before the students arrive," he was explaining. "That'll be sometime in early June, which should give you plenty of time to. . .well, to brush up, or whatever you might need to do to get ready. So, I'll talk with you soon, then."

"Yes, uh, thanks Mr. Crowley. I look forward to it."

"I'll call you. . .if it's all right," he said, as he turned and walked back behind his desk.

Oh, it's all right. . .definitely all right, she thought.

Patty felt his eyes watching her as she walked toward the door. She hoped Mrs. Parker or the other office staff members wouldn't notice her blush, but probably they would. He had said he would call her. Did that mean he would call to let her know when to report for the job? Or did it mean something else?

After picking up the forms from Mrs. Parker, Patty rushed out of the school building. Once outside, she ambled to her car in a daze, berating herself for her silly schoolgirl behavior, which no doubt had been so obvious to the man. How could she be so stupid?

Of course, he hadn't been nearly so subtle as he had thought, either. She could tell that he had also been attracted to her. After all, what about that half-hearted hint about her inviting him out to meet her father? Yes, she might just do that; she might do it real soon.

She wondered if she should have told him about Jenny. Of course, the subject had not come up. Patty was aware that single parents, especially women, were often shunned—and rightly so, she had to admit. Her first responsibility must always be to her daughter.

Why was she even thinking about all this? She had just interviewed with the assistant principal and he had offered her a job. Nothing further could come of that association—not if she wanted to maintain her new teaching position. Still.... Were there any regulations prohibiting teachers from having a relationship with an assistant principal, she wondered.

Yes, of course, stupid! That would be fraught with all kinds of dangers.

Patty drove home, still in her trance-like state, rationalizing that it was because she had taken her first step toward commencing what she had always wanted to do. Yet, deep down she knew her excitement was partly the result of the...*other*—however that *other* might be interpreted. She also knew she would see this man again, and the next time would not be in his office.

Chapter 21

Kirby didn't look at the paper the waitress had given him until after he left Denny's and was back inside his truck. Then unfolding the piece of paper, he glanced at it and smiled. Pulling his atlas from underneath the seat, he opened it to the state map of North Carolina. Rachel had indeed obtained the address: 2721 East Brow Lane, in a little town called Roan Creek.

Kirby was neither surprised nor terribly disappointed when he didn't find East Brow Lane listed in the index of the atlas. No doubt it was one of many small country roads, some known only by the people who lived in the immediate area. The small town of Roan Creek was barely on the map itself, appearing only as a black dot along Highway 19, about ten or fifteen miles northeast of Asheville. He vaguely remembered Patty having stated that the old man lived on a mountaintop, and since the name of the road was East Brow, Kirby decided the residence must be atop Roan Mountain, which according to the map was just beyond and to the west of the little town.

Kirby felt his spirits rise as he took the northern bypass around Asheville and exited onto a stretch of interstate heading north, which according to the map would take him to Highway 19, the small state road leading into the little town. He took another beer from the cooler, downed it in a couple of gulps, then flung the bottle at a road sign he was passing. He had no doubt that once he was in the town, he could stop and ask almost anyone how to get to East Brow Lane. Surely someone could direct him.

Now that he was within perhaps less than half an hour from his encounter, Kirby felt his muscles ripple and his pulse quicken. Again, he ran over in his mind how he would teach the woman and her tattletale daughter that they had messed with the wrong man. Kirby considered that the old man would probably be there and might intervene in an attempt to protect his daughter, but Kirby had no doubt of his ability to deal with him in short order. The day he had to worry about a fifty-something-year-old grandpa getting in his way was so far removed that Kirby couldn't even contemplate it.

A quick stop at a combination Exxon station and convenience store on the south end of town was all it took for Kirby to find out that he was only about five miles from his destination. The pimply-faced kid behind the counter told him that he needed to continue north on Highway 19 until he came to Highway 19W, which would take him to the top of the mountain. According to the kid, East Brow Lane was the first or second intersection after reaching the top.

Kirby headed up the crooked mountain road, hardly able now to contain his excitement and keep the Ford pickup at a speed slow enough to negotiate the sharp turns safely. Tires screamed as he went around the first horseshoe turn, and adrenaline flooded through him. His mouth almost watered as he neared his long awaited encounter, which had by now become such an obsession that he remained firmly focused on the task ahead.

He didn't slow until he passed through the gap at the top of the mountain. Directly ahead on the left he saw a road intersecting the highway, and as he got closer, he noticed a small green sign on a pole that leaned precariously, as if it might topple over at any moment. According to the sign, this was indeed East Brow Lane. He smiled to himself as he executed a left turn and headed up the narrow gravel road. Immediately, he saw a mailbox in front of the first house on the left. The address was 2715.

Just about there!

On the mailbox of the next house, Kirby noted the address was 2717. His heart beat faster. The next house he came to was still under construction and had no mailbox, consequently, no address. Now he could see the driveway of the house just beyond, which must surely be number 2721.

Nearly there . . .

Chapter 22

Snider's Family Restaurant was one of three *real* restaurants in the little town of Roan Creek, not counting the typical fast-food places that had cropped up nearly everywhere, such as McDonalds, Burger King and Pizza Hut. Of the two other restaurants, one served primarily fried chicken and hamburgers, and the quality of the food at the other had deteriorated to the point that only a select few ever ate there anymore.

Snider's Restaurant was in the heart of downtown, right across from the courthouse. The establishment had been there ever since I could remember. When I had lived here as a boy, the Snider family had actually owned and operated the restaurant, maintaining a quality of food and service that was unsurpassed anywhere in the county. The place had changed ownership a few times since then, but the name had remained the same, perhaps in an effort to maintain some of the old quality and goodwill that had developed through the years. Apparently this had worked, because the restaurant still flourished, drawing huge luncheon crowds and filling the private dining room with whatever luncheon or dinner meeting happened to be taking place. Today, the Chamber of Commerce was holding its monthly meeting in the dining room.

The young waitress approached our table, carrying two glasses of water and a couple of hand-printed pieces of paper listing the daily specials. For a single price of only $4.95, one had a choice of three entrees: hamburger steak, fried chicken, or ham steak, including biscuits or cornbread, and a choice of three vegetables from a group of about fifteen items. The price also included drink and dessert. From past experience, I knew that no matter which choice one selected, the food all tasted about the same—good, but still the taste was similar.

"What's the soup of the day, Rosie?" asked Sarah when the waitress had placed their water glasses in front of them.

"Vegetable beef, Miz Wallace. Had me a bowl earlier. It's real good."

"Hmmm. . .I think I'll have the soup and salad, then. . .and sweet tea."

"Yes, ma'am. And how 'bout you, sir?"

"I'll try the fried chicken. May as well be really bad, so give me the mashed potatoes and gravy, pinto beans and the squash casserole."

"Biscuits or cornbread?"

"Cornbread. . .and iced tea, unsweetened."

"Yes sir. It'll be right out."

Sarah and I had arranged to meet for lunch today when I called her about setting up a meeting for Patty at the school. I couldn't even remember who had first broached the subject—must have been Sarah, I concluded. Regardless, I had looked forward to seeing her, and now that we were here I found that, although I was a little nervous, I was enjoying her company immensely. She only had about an hour before she had to be back at school, and already I found myself wishing it could be longer.

Sarah *once*-Hartman Wallace had aged well. She still maintained her trim figure, and except for the gray hair, which she told me she refused to color because she had earned every one of them, she could have passed for a woman in her early-forties; although, according to my calculations, she must be about fifty-six or seven. I remembered that she had been a strawberry blond in high school. She had been popular then and was selected as a cheerleader for the two years I had known her in school. She was a small woman, about five-foot-two—and *eyes of blue*—as I always said to finish the sentence. She still had a pretty smile, her teeth nearly as white as they had ever been. A few wrinkles were evident around her eyes, but these only served to add character. Sarah's best feature was her warm smile, though, which lit up her whole face, her eyes sparkling like a seventeen-year-old.

"How's Jenny doing, Tom? Any progress?"

"Not really. I don't know what the problem is. The doctors say she should be walking by now, but she doesn't even seem to try."

"I'm sorry to hear that. Must be hard on you and Patty."

"Yeah, it is, especially Patty. She still blames herself. I just feel sort of helpless."

"I understand. How's that book coming along? Any inspiration, or have you had time to work on it?"

"Haven't had much chance for a while—but no inspiration, either. Guess I'll just have to put it on hold until . . ."

Sarah broke the silence. "I understand Patty made quite a splash at school the other day."

"Oh yeah? How'd you mean?"

"At her interview. I heard she had young Paul Crowley practically eating out of her hand. Everyone in the office was talking about how gorgeous she is—and nice, too. I caught a glimpse of her as she was leaving, and I'd have to agree."

"Takes after her mother," I said quickly, displaying a sheepish grin.

"Your face is turning red, Tom Carter."

"Just your imagination, Sarah."

"Is not!"

"Is too."

"So, is she going to take the job?"

"I don't know. She seems excited about it, and teaching's what she's always wanted to do. I hope she'll take it. I think it'd be good for her and Jenny to stay here and make a life. Am I being selfish?"

"Of course. . .but who wouldn't be? I hope it all works out."

We sat in silence for a few moments, during which Sarah nodded to a few people who passed by heading into the Chamber of Commerce luncheon. I didn't know any of them. It seemed a younger generation had taken over the management of the town, and in a way this made me feel sad. . .and even older.

Rosie soon arrived with our food and each of us worried over it for a few minutes. Finally, Sarah said, "It's good to see you again, Tom. With you, I feel. . .I don't know, *comfortable*, I guess is about as good a word as I can think of. That probably sounds real exciting, huh? Comfortable, like an old shoe, right?" She giggled and I winked at her.

"That's about the best compliment I've had in a long time, Sarah Hartman Wallace. I guess I could say ditto."

I came close then to inviting her out to my house for dinner. I'd been thinking about it for a long time, but wasn't sure how Patty would feel about it, and still wasn't sure I wanted to take the relationship to that level just yet either. Why was I so afraid?

"So, do you really think Patty's going to stay? Will they continue living with you if she does?"

What did she mean by that, I wondered? Was she fishing, or just making conversation? Probably the latter. "I don't know, Sarah. Right now we're just taking things a day at a time. I think Patty might just decide to stay if she has an opportunity to teach here—it's what she's always wanted to do. To be honest, she's had her share of troubles, primarily with the men in her life, since Jenny's father was killed. I think this kind of life might be just what the doctor ordered. I try not to tell her how to run her life, though. I've told her that she and Jenny can stay as long as they want. But if they decide to settle here, I'm sure Patty will want a place of her own as soon as she can get it. I don't blame her; I wouldn't want to live with a crotchety old man, either."

"Hmmm. . .crotchety old man, huh? That what you've become, Tom Carter?"

"Yeah, I guess so."

"Oh, I don't think so. I sort of like what you've become." Sarah lowered her head and smiled. "Oh my, I shouldn't have said that. The man might get the wrong idea and think I'm coming on to him," she said to her plate.

"I like what you've become, too, Sarah. How come we only ever had that one date, anyway? Or was it two?"

"Two, you devil! Don't you remember taking me to the football banquet your senior year?"

"Oh, yeah. I try to forget that night. That's the time I got sick and. . .well, let's not relive that experience—not while we're eating."

"Yeah, but you got over it. Don't you remember what happened on my front porch later on?"

"Uh. . .I kissed you with vomit-breath, right?"

"You were okay, by then. All that Juicy Fruit gum, I guess."

"You remember that?"

"I remember everything, Tom Carter. I'm hurt that you don't."

"I remember, Sarah. I remember."

"Not like I do, though. Your memory of those times doesn't include. . .well, I guess I've gone this far, I may as well say it. . .you remember me as a silly little girl, probably, and I remember you as . . ."

"As?"

"Don't push your luck, big boy?"

"You started it."

"Yeah, I guess I did. Okay, I remember you as. . .well, as someone who was very nice to me and. . .well, to be honest, I think I had a little bit of a crush on you."

"Really? I never knew that."

"I know. I never told anybody. . .especially you."

"Why not?"

"I don't know. I guess because you were beyond my reach then."

"And what about now?"

Sarah didn't answer for a few moments, then she shook her head, smiled and said, "Let's slow down a little, Tom. I don't want to rush into something that we're not both ready for. I want to be your friend first, and then if. . .well, if there's more, that would be great. But I don't want to jeopardize our friendship by trying to relive those schoolgirl fantasies. Agreed?"

"Okay. I guess you're right."

I finished my chicken breast and vegetables, then began on the dessert, which looked like pound cake with some sort of white icing. Casually, I asked, "You believe in magic, Sarah?"

"Magic? Of course, doesn't everyone?"

"No, I mean *really*?"

"Yes, I mean *really*, too. Of course, I believe in magic. It's all around us. Why do you ask?"

"Oh, I don't know. I've just been thinking of something that happened when I was a boy growing up here. Just silly stuff."

"Not *silly* stuff, Tom Carter. Obviously, you don't think so. Wanna tell me about it?"

"I don't know. Maybe sometime. . .but not now. I'm still trying to figure it all out myself."

"Okay. I have one for you, then. Do you believe in angels?"

"Angels? Why do you ask?"

"Why'd you ask if I believed in magic?"

"Okay, you got me there. Angels, huh?"

"Uh-huh."

"I don't think so."

"What! They're all around us, you know. You really don't believe in angels? Yet, you believe in magic?"

"I never said I believed in magic. I just asked you if you did."

"Ah, the old cop-out."

"How about a cup of coffee, Sarah? Got time?"

"Maybe for one, if we hurry."

I got Rosie's attention and she brought us each a cup of coffee. We sat sipping the hot liquid, each seemingly absorbed in our own thoughts.

Finally, I said, "Uh, Sarah?

"Yes, Tom?"

"How'd you like to. . .how'd you like to come out to the house for dinner sometime soon? You know, get to know Patty and meet my granddaughter. I mean, if you and Patty are going to be teaching together, you ought to get to know one another."

She smiled. "I thought you'd never ask."

"Well, I better check with Patty first, since she's the cook. I'll call you and let you know when, okay?"

"Uh-huh. Promises, promises."

"I *will* call, I promise."

Sarah glanced at her watch. "As much as I hate to leave, Tom, I have to get back to school. I have. . .well, I've enjoyed this more than. . .more than you could know." She lowered her head and quickly added, "I'm sorry, it's just. . .well, I don't get out much anymore—not with people I care about, anyway. Oh, my, I'm digging myself in deeper, aren't I?"

"No, Sarah. I feel the same. This has been. . .well, wonderful. Let's do it again, and soon. I'll check with Patty and I'll call you in a day or so, okay?"

"Okay, if you're sure."

"Nothing's sure, Sarah. That's what makes it fun."

"If you say so, Tom Carter. I have to go or I'll be late. Thanks for lunch."

"It was your idea."

"Was it?"

"I don't know. Does it matter?"

"Not really. I'll talk with you soon, Tom."

"Okay."

As I headed up the mountain, I couldn't help replaying portions of our conversation. What did it all mean? I hoped Patty wouldn't be too upset that I'd invited Sarah to dinner—well, promised to invite her, anyway. I didn't think she would mind, though. Actually, I thought Sarah and Patty would get along splendidly—at least, I found himself hoping they would. So, I had taken that first monumental step now: inviting the woman to dinner. After that, it was only a short leap to. . .to *what*? I had to admit I was attracted to her, and was nearly certain she was also attracted to me. No, I was more than *nearly* certain of it, I admitted, and that thought frightened me even more.

Chapter 23

As he approached the house, Kirby noticed a white, new-looking Dodge Caravan in the driveway. Had he been given bad information? He had expected to see Patty's blue van, although it was possible this vehicle belonged to her old man. Maybe hers was in the garage, or she could be out somewhere. He slowed to give himself time to evaluate this unexpected situation. If she wasn't here, he didn't want to alert her old man to his presence. She had no doubt told the old man a bunch of lies and even if she hadn't, he would not welcome Kirby warmly. Still, if he had to encounter grandpa first, with her not here, then Kirby might jeopardize his chance of surprising her, which was one of his primary advantages.

As he crept along, trying to decide what to do, Kirby noticed an old lady walking down the road toward him. She was just passing the corner of the yard in front of the house he had assumed was his destination. The old woman was dressed in a faded, flowery house dress and wore an ill-fitting black cardigan sweater. As she ambled along, her shoulders slumped, Kirby noticed a big black Labrador retriever trailing along behind her. Just for a moment, he admired the sleek, handsome animal.

Kirby was now close enough to see the house number on the mailbox: 2721, as expected.

Yes! This is the place. His heart beat faster.

He had to make a quick decision now whether to turn into the driveway or continue on past. As he approached close enough to see beyond the van in the driveway, he glanced toward the house and noticed a little girl sitting on the front porch. Yes, this had to be the place, because he was nearly certain that was the girl—the kid who had gotten him into this whole mess in the first place. He smiled as he thought again of how he would make her sorry she hadn't listened to his advice about not telling anyone what he'd done.

Kirby noticed that the old woman and the dog were now directly in front of the yard. She had stopped near the mailbox and was staring at his truck as he turned into the driveway. He slid to a halt behind the white van, still wondering why the blue Caravan was nowhere in sight. Looking toward the porch again, Kirby confirmed that this definitely was the girl sitting there on the porch. He noticed now that she was sitting in some sort of wheelchair, and briefly Kirby wondered why—although what difference did it make?

Jumping out of his truck, Kirby headed toward the porch. With dripping sarcasm, and dragging out his words for effect, Kirby announced, "Da. . .deeeee's home," as he approached the kid, who began struggling to back away.

I remained in high spirits as I continued up the mountain. I had been more than a little apprehensive about this luncheon with Sarah, although I still didn't know why I felt that way.

Certainly, it had gone better than I might have expected. Still, I was somewhat concerned about my impulsive promise of a dinner invitation, worrying that I should have at least discussed it with Patty first.

My euphoric disposition heightened until by the time I turned onto East Brow, I couldn't help feeling that everything was going to work out well, even including Jenny's problem. I rarely experienced these elated feelings anymore, where everything in life seemed bright and sunny—even including the weather, which today was warm with a near-cloudless, deep blue sky. Suddenly I felt like a silly teenager with a crush on a new girl I'd just met, causing all things to seem well with the world.

Approaching the driveway, I noticed Clara Wilson standing statue-like, staring toward my house, her big black Lab standing beside her, also looking toward the house, its ears pointed forward. I imagined Clara might be considering whether to go up to the porch to see Jenny, whom I assumed might be sitting out there enjoying the sunny, spring day.

When I got closer, I noticed the red pickup truck parked in my driveway, behind Patty's new van. Not recognizing the vehicle, I tried to imagine who it might be. I waved to Mrs. Wilson, but the old lady ignored me and continued to stare toward the house, causing me to begin to feel uneasy.

As I turned into the driveway, I noticed the Tennessee license plates on the truck. For just a moment, I was confused, but glancing toward the porch, I suddenly understood exactly what was going on. Reaching down beside my seat, I grabbed the nightstick, which I had carried for years, never expecting to have to use it. Now, perhaps I would.

Clara Wilson had stopped in her tracks when she noticed the red truck slowly making its way up the road. Something was wrong, bad wrong about this situation; she just felt it in her bones. As the truck proceeded toward her, then slowed and turned into the driveway, the big Lab seemed to sense Clara's anxiety and flattened his ears back against his head. Then, when the man got out of the truck, the dog's ears pointed forward and he and the old lady each stood frozen, watching as the man approached the porch. Yes, something was definitely wrong here, Clara decided. Absent-mindedly, she patted the big Lab on the head and he started whining, as if uncertain what to do and awaiting a command from his master.

When the man got near the porch, the hair on the back of the dog's neck stood on end and his whine developed into a low, deep growl. Clara shuddered in dread of what was surely about to happen, although she did not yet know exactly what it might be. She thought it strange that she hadn't foreseen this. She then saw Carter's Explorer heading up the road and she breathed a little easier, certain that Carter would be able to handle whatever was about to happen. Still, she knew it was going to be bad.

The events of the next few seconds took place so rapidly and nearly simultaneously that Clara stood frozen in position, observing the events unfolding before her in a blur, as if watching the finale of a three-ring circus.

First, Jenny seemed to recognize the bad man who was rushing toward her. As he came closer, the little girl started screaming and trying to back away. "No! Get away! Don't touch me! Mommy! Mommy! Help!"

At about that time, Carter slid to a halt, jerked open his car door and ran toward the porch. Clara noticed he had some sort of stick in his hand. Apparently hearing Jenny's screaming, he picked up his pace. Clara hoped he could stop the bad man before he hurt her Jenny.

Just then the front door opened and the little girl's mother rushed out. She hesitated for a moment, a look of shock appeared on her face, and then she dashed across the porch and positioned herself between the man and her little girl.

Suddenly the big Lab bolted. Clara tried to yell at him to stop, but no sound came forth. The dog bounded across the yard, then flew through the air, landing full force against the bad man's shoulder, knocking him away from the little girl. The man crashed to the ground on his back between the walkway and the front porch, the big dog landing on top. Clara could hear Omega as he began snarling, biting and tearing at the man. She watched, frozen in position, as the dog began shaking its head from side to side, tearing at the man's arms and clothing, trying to get at his throat. The man flailed his arms, attempting to ward off the crazed animal. Clara heard him scream in pain as the dog continued to tear at his flesh. She knew she should try to stop

Omega, but she just couldn't make herself do anything. The bad man was trying to hurt her Jenny and good ole Omega was going to stop him.

Jenny continued to scream and now the mother was screaming too. At about that time, Carter reached the melee. He stood just long enough for Clara to wonder if he was going to allow the dog to kill the man, then he began hitting the dog across its flank with the stick, not hard enough to hurt the animal, just hard enough to divert its attack. Clara hoped he wouldn't hurt her Omega as she watched the big dog back away a few feet. She could still hear him growling as he darted toward the man on the ground, then backed away, looking back and forth between the bad man and the man holding the stick.

Carter then jumped astride the man on the ground, the stick raised above his head. She heard him yell, "What the hell do you think you're doing? I ought to break this across your head!"

The bad man raised his hands to ward off the blow, while the woman grabbed the handles of Jenny's wheelchair and dragged her back beside the front door. She then ran over toward the two men.

"No, Dad! Don't hit him! Let him up. I—I'll handle this."

Carter slowly climbed off the man on the ground and moved far enough to the side so the man could sit up. Clara could see blood running down the bad man's arms as he slowly struggled to his feet. She watched as he glanced back and forth between the dog, which was crouched nearby, its teeth bared and a low growl rumbling from its throat, and Carter, who also stood nearby, his stick still at the ready.

The woman then grabbed the dazed man by the arm, dragged him away from the porch and out into the front yard, where she began yelling at him and waving her finger in his face. The dog moved along with them and stood crouched nearby, teeth still bared, a low growl emanating from deep within its throat. The big Lab watched every move the man made, apparently ready to strike again if he felt his services were needed. Carter moved about halfway between the porch and where Patty and the man stood, his stick held at his side.

"Damned dog nearly killed me!" yelled the bad man. "You people are all crazy!"

The dog moved closer, its fangs bared. Its growl deepened as it watched the man and woman arguing. The man then backed away, holding his bleeding arms against his shirt. Patty continued to yell at him, as he eased back toward his truck, carefully inching away from the dog.

"Don't come crying to me, bitch!" he yelled at the woman. "I never wanna see you again—any of you! You're all crazy! Damned dog attacking an unarmed, harmless man like that!"

The woman yelled something at him and the man then turned and sprinted toward his truck. The big Lab bolted at the same time, nipping at the man's heels as he jumped in the truck. He slammed the door and started the engine, then backed hard into the Explorer that was parked behind him, knocking it back a few feet. He then moved forward again and banged into the back of the new Caravan.

Reversing again, he turned the wheel so that he backed out at an angle, just missing the Explorer as he turned into the yard. Tires spun on the grass and dug into the soft earth as the truck turned in a tight circle across the front yard. It then skidded into the road, nearly running down Clara Wilson, who still stood frozen in position near the edge of the yard.

Clara watched in a daze as the red truck disappeared down the street, the big Lab giving chase.

Patty took Jenny into the bedroom and lay on the bed with her, holding the little in her arms until finally she stopped crying and fell asleep. Then she came back into the living room and sat on the couch beside her father.

"Is she okay?" asked Tom. "That bastard didn't hurt her, did he?"

"No...not physically. She was pretty shaken, but she's asleep now...which is probably the best thing for her. I'll talk with her later about all this. Dad, I never expected him to come...I—I'm so sorry I caused all this trouble."

"This wasn't your fault, Patty. By the way, what'd you say to him to make him leave so suddenly? You think I should call the sheriff?"

"No, I don't think Kirby will cause us any more problems. I just pointed out to him what his choices were. And I'm sure he knew I meant it."

"What did you tell him, Patty?"

"Just that he could stay here and be arrested for assault, both sexual and physical—assuming of

course that you or I didn't decide to kill him first—
or that he could leave now and never, ever come
near me or Jenny again."

"It looked like he took you seriously, the way
he took off like that."

"Oh, yeah, I'm sure he did! He knows me well
enough to know when I mean business. Kirby's not
really such a bad guy, Dad—most of the time. I
wouldn't have stayed with him so long otherwise.
It's just that when he's been drinking he gets. . .well,
you can imagine, I guess.

"Well, I don't reckon I have to imagine!"

"I think he just came down here to make his
point that I couldn't. . .well, you know how some
guys are. He couldn't stand to let me get away with
hurting his ego by just leaving him the way I did.
He's made his point now, so I don't think we'll ever
hear from him again."

"Well, I sure hope you're right, Patty. I should've
let the dog finish taking care of him. Well, I guess I
couldn't just let it kill him—but I sure felt like it.
Felt like killing him myself, scaring Jenny that
way."

"No, you did the right thing, Dad. Otherwise,
he'd be the victim and you'd be the one going to
jail."

"Yeah, you're probably right about that. Wonder
why that dog just attacked him like that, anyway?
Think it sensed he was about to hurt Jenny?"

"I don't know...maybe. Some dogs are protective
that way, I guess, especially when it comes to
children. Who knows, maybe Clara sent him in for
the attack."

"Hmmm...maybe so. Guess we need to thank her, in any case."

"I know. I'll talk with her later. I want to let her know how sorry I am for the way I've been treating her. I think I'll invite her over for dinner soon. I'm sure Jenny would like that."

Patty spent a long time with Jenny later that evening, trying to explain what had happened and why. She assured her daughter that she need not be afraid of Kirby anymore, and promised that she was never going back to him, and that she was sure he would never come here again. She imagined it would take a long time for Jenny to get over this, but Patty intended to devote all her time and energy to helping her daughter with her recovery, both physical and emotional.

Later, Patty cried herself to sleep. For the first time, she felt the full impact of what she had done to Jenny...not so much the car wreck but the emotional injuries she had caused by her poor choice of men. She made up her mind that nothing like this would ever again come between her and her beautiful little girl.

Oh, God, please forgive me. . .and please find a way for Jenny to be able to walk again. Make me crippled, if that's what it takes. . .but please, God, let her walk again.

Chapter 24

A gibbous moon was just peeking over the horizon across the valley when Clara Wilson opened her front door to let in the group of dogs that would spend the night inside with her tonight. The evening was exceptionally warm, with just a touch of a westerly breeze. Next door, the Peterson's halogen motion-sensor light on the corner of their house suddenly came on, bathing Clara's front yard and shining into her eyes. She cursed to herself, wishing that damned light would break into a thousand pieces. She considered throwing a rock at it, but doubted she could hit it. The light sometimes came on at odd hours throughout the night, especially when the wind was blowing the leaves, causing enough motion to activate the sensor. It shone brightly into her window, and when she was outside, the light prevented her from enjoying the moon and stars in a darkened sky, as they were meant to be viewed. And these people thought she was the crazy one.

The dogs came to her as she called their names: first Perky, the little Beagle, then Kip, the Cocker Spaniel. They wagged their tails, panted and jumped on her. She petted each and made them sit and wait until she had them all assembled.

"Omega, come boy," Clara called. She waited a few moments, but the big Lab did not appear. She looked all around the yard but couldn't see him anywhere. "Omega, where are you? Come boy. Time to come inside."

Still, Omega did not appear.

Clara walked all the way around her house, calling his name. Nothing. As she passed Gordy's grave, she stopped and looked down. Sadness overcame her and she stood silently for a few moments. Then she began to cry.

Poor Gordy.

Clara didn't know how long she stood there.

Poor Clara, she thought. Now her Omega was gone too. What was she to do? He had gotten out once before, but had come back a few minutes after she'd noticed he was gone. Perhaps he had gotten out again; maybe he would return soon.

But what if something had happened to him? What if he didn't come back at all?

The motion sensor light had finally shut off and moonlight created a warm glow across the yard. Still, it was too dark for Clara to see now without a light, so she left Gordy's graveside and hurried inside. Grabbing her flashlight, she ran back outside. She had to find him. How could she bear another loss?

"Omega! Omega!" she called as she opened the front gate and headed down the lane toward the main road. Clara remembered those two she-devil dogs down at that house near the highway and wondered if Omega might be down there. Probably one of the bitches was in heat again and he'd gone down there to service her. Damn him if he had! She would kill him if she caught him with one of those bitches again. Maybe she'd kill the bitch, too.

She quickened her pace, although her arthritic joints sent seething pains up and down her legs and through her hips and back. She could hardly see, even with the flashlight. Carter must have gotten her a cheap one, because it didn't seem to be making much light. As she passed Carter's house, she looked in that direction, but could only see a faint light shining through the front window. Probably they were in the back watching TV. Damn that woman, claiming to be Jenny's mother. It wasn't fair that she got to spend time with Jenny and Clara didn't.

Clara knew why the woman didn't want her to see Jenny. *She thinks I'm crazy, just like all the others. Does she really think I would hurt my Jenny?* The bad man had tried to hurt her, but he was gone now. They should be thanking Clara for that, since her dog had risked his life to help the little girl.

When Clara arrived in front of the house down near the highway, she didn't see or hear any dogs. Shining her flashlight into the driveway and all around, she couldn't see her Omega anywhere. She called his name, softly for fear of arousing suspicion of the people who lived there. Sure that they already thought her crazy, she imagined they might shoot her if they found her bumbling around in their yard after dark. Of course, they might call the sheriff and have her put away, probably in one of those places where they kept crazy people. Clara would rather die than to go to one of those places.

Seeing Omega nowhere around, Clara continued down toward the main road, which was less than a hundred yards away. As she neared the highway, she stopped and listened.

She heard a faint noise. It sounded like a dog whining—an injured dog, Clara deduced, based on her vast experience with and connection to members of the canine family.

Oh, no, please don't let it be him—not my Omega.

Could he have been hit by a car and was lying there alongside the road, begging for help?

Clara tried to run, but she fell, scraping her knees on the gravel. Scrambling to her feet, she hobbled toward the whining sounds, which she was certain now were those of an injured dog. It might not be Omega, of course. Maybe it was one of the bitches. Maybe one of the bitches had been hit by a car. Well, good riddance if that was true. No, this wasn't Omega, Clara decided, because surely she would recognize his cry. No, it couldn't possibly be him.

As she approached the source of the sound, Clara came upon a ditch next to the highway. Shining her dim light down into the ditch, she saw the dog and her old heart nearly stopped. It was the big Labrador, Omega. When the beam of her flashlight caught his eye, she detected his pleading look of suffering. He tried to wag his tail, but it appeared his whole backside was crushed. Clawing desperately with his front paws, he tried to get to her, his whining becoming a mournful cry, pleading for her to help him.

Clara nearly fainted. She had to help him, yet what could she do? She went to him, knelt beside him and gently rubbed his head. He licked at her fingers, and cried.

"My baby, my poor, sweet baby," Clara moaned, trying to soothe him

She continued to stroke the big dog's head and then she ran her hand down his back. When she reached his flank, the poor animal screamed in agony.

"Poor, poor baby. Mommy's gonna take care of you. Mommy will make you well. Don't cry. It's gonna be all right. Clara's gonna help her baby."

The big Lab continued to whimper as Clara ran over in her mind what to do. There really was no choice. She had to get him to the vet. But first she had to get down the mountain to Roan Creek. She had taken a couple of her other dogs to the vet down there during the past year. He seemed like such a nice man, always treating her babies as if they were important. Of course, his office wouldn't be open at this time of night. She remembered that he lived nearby, though, so she would just find his house and get him to fix her Omega.

Gotta do it. Gotta go get the car. Gotta help my poor baby.

Clara hadn't driven her old car in several days. She remembered now that the last time she tried to start it, the engine had barely turned over enough to get going. The 1973 Oldsmobile was getting old and weak, just like its owner. Soon it would probably die, too. She had meant to get it fixed.

Leaning forward, Clara hugged the crying animal and whispered, "Mommy'll be right back, baby. Gotta go get the car so I can take my baby to the doctor."

Clara rushed up the road as fast as she could, heading toward her house. As she passed Carter's place, she briefly considered stopping and knocking on the door. Maybe he would help her get her baby down to the doctor. She didn't want to be a bother, though, so she wouldn't ask him; she would just do this herself. She didn't want to be beholden to him anymore. They had forbidden her to see Jenny. Probably Carter had even conspired with the woman who thought she was Jenny's mother to ensure that Clara could never see the little girl again. No, she wouldn't ask those horrible people to help her do anything. She could do it all by herself.

Once inside her house Clara fumbled in her purse for the car keys. But they weren't there! She panicked, ran into her bedroom, looked all around. No keys! Then she began jerking out drawers. Still no keys. In a frenzy, she ran back into the living room, looking around wildly, her old heart nearly jumping out of her chest. What was she going to do?

Suddenly she remembered the hook by the door. Stumbling across the room, she reached the hook and grabbed the keys. Then she ran out the door and headed toward the Oldsmobile, which she'd left parked beside the house. She jumped in, fumbled to get the key in the ignition. The engine turned over slowly, grinding . . .grinding, turning over slower and slower. It had to start! It had to!

With a loud rumble, the old engine finally came to life. It revved to near maximum RPM as she held the accelerator pressed to the floor. Finally releasing the accelerator, she shoved the gear lever into reverse and backed quickly down the driveway toward the gate. Unable to see behind her, she allowed the car to drift over into the yard. Suddenly she felt it crash into a small tree. Slamming the gear lever into drive, she pressed the accelerator and the car leapt forward. Then putting it into reverse, she turned the wheel and backed toward the gate again. Cursing herself now for not having remembered to open the gate first, she stopped the car, jumped out and dragged the gate open. Then she got back into the car, backed out into the street, then sped blindly down the lane toward the highway.

Sliding to a halt next to the main road, Clara put the car in reverse, turned the wheel and backed over to a position as close to the ditch as she dared. Leaving the engine running, she got out and ran over to Omega, who still lay there crying. She struggled to lift the big dog, but couldn't pick him up. Glancing wildly around in the moonlight, Clara tried to decide what to do.

"Sorry, Baby. I ain't got no choice. I know this is gonna hurt."

Taking the big Lab by his front paws, Clara struggled to pull him across the grass and up the side of the ditch toward her car, using strength she didn't know she possessed. The dog cried in pain, but didn't protest too much, almost as if he were aware that she had no other choice.

When she had him beside her car, she opened the back door and pulled with all her might, trying to get his front quarters up onto the seat. Then she got behind him and shoved, knowing the pain this would cause the poor baby. The big dog yelped and screamed, but then began pulling with his front paws, clawing at the upholstery. Finally, with his help, she got him inside the car. After closing the door, Clara ran around to the driver's side and got in. She gunned the engine, causing tires to spin on the gravel, and then squeal as they reached the pavement.

Heading down the mountain as fast as she dared, Clara squinted, attempting to keep the old car in the road. The car weaved back and forth across the centerline as if its driver was drunk. Able only to see the dark silhouettes of trees whizzing past on either side of the road, she aimed the car generally between these shapes. Fortunately, there was no other traffic at this time of night.

Approaching the first horseshoe turn, she braked hard and the car skidded, its rear end sliding onto the shoulder of the road. Loose gravel clanged underneath the car as it slid toward the bluff. Jerking the wheel, Clara fought the skid with all her might, trying to turn in the direction she was skidding, as she seemed to remember was the correct response. Suddenly, the rear end of the car careened back onto the pavement and tires screeched as the Olds fishtailed a couple of times. Clara continued to fight the steering wheel until the car finally straightened out. Then she turned the wheel first one way and then the other, trying to keep the old car in the road.

Approaching the second horseshoe turn, Clara suddenly was blinded by the bright lights of an oncoming vehicle. She hit her brakes and fought the wheel, hoping she could hold the car steady until the other vehicle had gone past. Suddenly the other car whizzed by, coming within inches of sideswiping her. As Clara's eyes tried to adjust to the dimmer light now, she strained to determine whether she was about to enter the next horseshoe curve. She had taken her foot off the brake and now her car was again picking up speed.

When Omega whimpered loudly from the back seat, Clara turned her head to check on him. In that instant, her car left the road and flew over the cliff. Becoming airborne, the big Olds sailed through the air, toward the rocks more than a hundred feet below.

They found what was left of the Oldsmobile the following morning, upside-down at the bottom of the cliff. When the rescue squad finally got down to the car, they discovered the body of an old woman. An injured Labrador lay across her, gently licking the blood from her face. Before they could get either the woman or the dog out of the car, the dog joined the woman in the hereafter.

Jenny cried for hours when we had to tell her about Clara's death. She lay on her bed with her kitten, refusing to talk to anyone, or even to eat. On the previous day, I had found another note in the mailbox. The message had been so strange that I decided not to read it to Jenny then, but now I wondered if perhaps I should. Maybe it might mean something to her.

Sitting beside her on the bed, I said, "Sweetheart, I found this note for you from Clara. Do you want me to read it?"

"Uh-huh," she whimpered, turning her head toward him and wiping her eyes with her sleeve.

"It says, 'Jenny. Time for me to go soon. Remember the angel I told you about. She'll come to you in a dream. She'll tell you what to do. Never forget me. I love you, child. Clara.'"

Jenny sobbed for a long time. Then she asked me to help her into her wheelchair. She said she was hungry.

A couple of days later, Jenny, Jenny and I stood out in the road watching, along with a few of the other neighbors, while some people from the animal shelter came to the Wilson house to take away the multitude of dogs and cats. The onlookers murmured and shook their heads as they watched while men rounded up twenty-seven dogs from the yard and three others from inside. Then the people watched as they removed eighteen cats from inside the house.

"They said she died instantly," said one of the ladies who lived up the street. "Said they found one of her old dogs in the car with her, but it died before they could get it out."

"She couldn't see to drive at night, you know," Mrs. Peterson from next door added. "She should've asked somebody to help her."

"Well, you know how crazy she was," added another woman.

"Yeah. At least, we won't have to listen to those barking dogs anymore!"

"Right!"

"I heard she had a daughter," another women said. "Reckon anybody's notified her?"

"Oh, I'm sure somebody has. I don't know where she lives anyway, do you?"

"No, and besides, it's none of our business," said the other woman.

Chapter 25

"Thanks for asking, Paul. I'd be happy to come down to the school and speak to the drama department," I replied to the assistant principal, as we sat around the table in the dining area.

"Great! I'll set it up then, and let you know soon."

"More chicken, Paul," Patty asked.

"Oh, no thanks. It was delicious, though."

"Yes, it was wonderful," Sarah said, looking at Patty and smiling.

"Told you she was a great cook," I said, smiling first at Patty, then at Sarah.

Three weeks had passed since Clara Wilson's accident. I was glad Patty had suggested she invite the assistant principal to dinner, along with Sarah. Somehow, having someone else there too seemed less threatening, although I still wasn't sure why I was so concerned about having Sarah to dinner at my house.

Fortunately, Jenny seemed to like both Sarah and Paul. Patty and I had worried that she might act withdrawn with them, refusing even to allow them to get to know her, but it had turned out the opposite. Both Sarah and Paul had brought presents for Jenny; Sarah's was a small case of Barbie clothes, and Paul had brought her a book about kittens. I had noticed the tears in Patty's eyes as she watched Jenny opening the gifts. I had also noticed the obvious attraction between my daughter and Paul Crowley. I wondered if they detected a similar attraction between Sarah and me. I was also pleased that Patty and Sarah seemed to be hitting it off so well. All in all, this dinner party was turning out much better than I had expected it might.

Patty had finally decided to accept the teaching position at the high school, and would be starting classes in a couple of weeks. The only cloud hanging over the otherwise happy occasion was Jenny's continual refusal to make any effort to learn to walk again. It seemed she had accepted that she would remain in the wheelchair indefinitely. I only hoped that when the realization set in with Jenny that she and Patty were going to remain here, at least for a year it seemed, then Jenny would no longer see moving back as an obstacle, assuming that was the reason she refused to try to walk.

"Coffee's ready," Patty announced. "Who wants a cup?"

Everyone except Jenny raised their hand, so Patty poured the coffee and distributed cream and sugar to those who wanted it. She also cut the pound cake Sarah had brought and set a generous piece in front of each.

"Mommy says you're gonna be my principal next year," Jenny said to Paul Crowley as he sipped his coffee.

Paul smiled at the little girl. "Yes, that's right, Jenny. I'll be accepting the position of principal at the grammar school starting next year. Quite a promotion. I'm really looking forward to it. You'll be in third grade, right?"

"That's right. Is it gonna be hard?"

"No, of course not. Not for a bright little girl like you," Paul said warmly.

"Do they let kids in wheelchairs go to school there?" Jenny asked, screwing up her face into her patented puzzled look.

"Well, of course. You don't worry about a thing. After all, I'm going to be the boss, so you can bet I'll make sure it won't be a problem," Paul said, his blue eyes flashing as he reached across and patted Jenny on the arm. Patty looked at him appreciatively and he winked at her.

After a few moments of silence, Sarah said, "So, how's the book coming along, Tom?"

"Yes, tell us about it," Paul suggested.

"Not much to tell, I'm afraid. Still can't seem to get past that first chapter. Guess I don't know where I'm going with it, or I'm not inspired. . .or both. Probably it'll take a miracle to get me going again."

"Well, miracles do happen," Sarah said. "What about that magic you asked me if I believed in, Tom Carter?"

"Oh, yeah. . .I forgot. And what about the angels you said you believed in?" I asked, winking at Jenny.

"I believe in angels," Jenny said, matter-of-factly.

"Well, so do I, sweetheart," Sarah said, smiling at Jenny and punching me in the side. "I bet your Old Pa does too."

"Mrs. Wilson believed in angels," Jenny said.

"Oh, did she?" Sarah said.

"Yes, and she told me how they sometimes come to people in dreams. Do you think that's true, Mrs. Wallace?"

"Well, who's to say how they come to you, Jenny. But you know, I'm convinced they're all around us just about all the time, don't you think?"

"Yes, I know they are. Clara told me so, and she knew all about such things."

"Yes, I'll bet she did," Sarah said.

After dinner, Jenny said she was tired, so following goodnight kisses all around, Patty took her daughter and put her to bed. Returning from the bedroom a few minutes later, Patty said, "She was one tired little girl. She's already asleep." Glancing first at Sarah, then resting her eyes on Paul, she said, "Thank you all for being so nice to her."

"She's a doll," Paul said.

"Thank you," Patty replied. "She's not always so easy to manage, I'm afraid."

"Guess that could apply to us all," Sarah added, looking at me.

"Why are you looking at me when you say that, Sarah Wallace?"

"Oh, did you think I was referring to you, Tom? I'm sorry." Sarah winked at Patty.

"Uh-huh. Well, weren't you?"

"If the shoe fits . . ."

We all laughed, then I suggested brandy and got up and served a snifter to all but Patty, who never drank.

After finishing the brandy, Paul said he should be going, and Sarah said that since she had an early day tomorrow, she should be leaving too. Patty walked Paul outside while Sarah and I said our good-byes inside.

"Well, how'd you think it turned out," I asked Patty after our guests had departed.

"Perfect, don't you think? I'm so happy everyone seemed to get along so well. Jenny seemed to like Paul, don't you think. He's soooo nice, isn't he?"

"Yeah, I guess he's okay," I said, winking. "Sure has steely blue eyes! What about Sarah? You two seemed to hit it off."

"Oh, she's nice too, Dad. Has green eyes, though." Patty smiled at me and added, "I'm so happy for you, Dad. I think you two make a perfect couple."

"Not so fast, darling daughter! I just asked the lady to dinner, not to marry me."

"Yeah, well...so far, that is. Looked to me like you two have a little more going than that."

"Oh, really? Is it that obvious? I was thinking the same thing about you and Paul. He looks a lot like his father. The elder Crowley was a star baseball pitcher when we were in high school. Had all the girls falling all over him. Never could figure out why. Must've been those steely blue eyes—sort of like his son, I guess."

"Oh, Dad."

For the first time since I had moved here, I felt as if I belonged. Now that it seemed Patty and Jenny would be settling here, the only thing that could have made me happier would be Jenny regaining the use of her legs. I still worried day and night about her and why she wouldn't even try to walk. If Patty's theory that Jenny wasn't walking because she was afraid that if she did they would have to move back to Knoxville, then perhaps before long she would allow herself to begin learning to walk again. I could only pray that she would.

As I lay in bed that evening, I allowed my mind to drift to Sarah, and wondered what, if anything, might become of our relationship. Briefly, our earlier conversation about angels being all around flashed through my consciousness. A faint picture of the tree appeared in my mind as he drifted off to sleep.

Chapter 26

"We have to go back!" Jenny resolutely announced the following morning during breakfast.

"Back? Back where, Jenny?" asked Patty, looking questioningly at her daughter.

"Back to where Ole Pa used to live!" Jenny said, her tone of voice sounding as if they should know exactly what she was talking about.

Patty glanced toward me and frowned. "What do you mean, Jenny?"

"I know, I know, I should've told you, Patty," I said, nodding and assuming a serious look.

Patty's frown deepened. Emphasizing each word, she said, "Should have told me what, Dad?"

"Ole Pa showed me where his old house used to be, Mommy," Jenny explained. "But it's gone now."

"Oh, okay...I guess," Patty said, her eyebrows raised as she looked at me, awaiting further explanation.

"I just wanted to show her where I lived when I was a little boy about her age. We drove by the other day while we were waiting for you to finish your hair appointment."

"Oh, I see. Well, okay, that doesn't sound like such a big deal? I mean. . .I'm just surprised you didn't say anything about it, Dad. Something going on I should know about?"

"Well, I meant to tell you, Patty. I'm sorry, I guess it just didn't seem important," I explained, hating having to lie to my daughter.

"We have to go back, Ole Pa! We have to!"

"Why, Jenny? The old house is gone now," I explained. "Why do you want to go back there?"

"We just have to, Ole Pa. Pleeease. We've gotta go back."

Why was Jenny so determined to go back, I wondered. Could it be she wanted me to push her in the swings again? Surely it had to be more than that. The pleading tone in her voice seemed to indicate this was something more significant. But what?

Patty looked at her daughter. "Jenny, what's so important about seeing where Old Pa's house used to be? Especially if you've already seen it. . .and the house isn't even there anymore."

I said, "Jenny, if you want me to take you back and push you in the swings again, maybe sometime we could—"

"No! You don't understand! I had a dream..." Jenny said.

"A dream?" Patty and I spoke simultaneously.

"Yes, and she...she told me to go look again."

"*She*?" questioned Patty. "*She*, who? Mrs. Wilson?"

"No! Not Mrs. Wilson, Mommie! *She*. . .you know...the angel!"

"The angel?" Patty and I repeated, exchanging questioning looks.

"Uh-huh. The angel told me to go back!"

Patty looked incredulously at her daughter, then back at me.

"Just like Clara said she would. Don't you understand? We have to go back!" Jenny demanded.

"Mrs. Wilson told you. . .an angel. . .in your dream?" I mumbled. "You mean the notes she kept leaving for you?"

"No, not that...in my dream, she told me to go back. Can we go now, pleeeease?"

Suddenly I began to experience a strange sensation. I felt a lump forming in my throat and tears came into my eyes. I didn't know what to do. Should we take Jenny back down the mountain and risk her being disappointed? Actually, I didn't see now that we had much choice.

By the time we finished breakfast, I had decided there was no good reason to go back, and again tried to convince Jenny it would be a waste of time. When Jenny started sobbing softly, ourr hearts melted, and we both quickly rationalized that it couldn't hurt to take Jenny for a ride, if that would placate her. She had seemed to have such fun swinging, maybe we could do that again, this time with Patty there to share the experience. I didn't expect anything more to come of it, but what could it hurt? Jenny seemed so adamant that we had to go back. Surely she must have had a dream about some angel or something that had caused her to feel this way. Or maybe something in those notes Clara Wilson had left caused Jenny to feel this way. Whatever it was, I could only hope that we would not be disappointed again, although I could not imagine how this venture could otherwise end up.

Jenny was all smiles as we headed down the mountain. By the time we reached the valley, I was again allowing second thoughts about how this could only end in disappointment to come to the fore. The best thing would be to turn around and go home.

As once more I tried to explain to Jenny that this was a waste of time, she again stated emphatically, "Ole Pa! We have to go and find it! The angel told me!"

"Find *IT*? Find what, Jenny?" asked Patty.

"The *tree*! Don't you see, we have to go and find the *magic tree*! Just like the angel said."

"Jenny, what in the world are you talking about?" Patty asked, looking at me.

"Well, uh...perhaps I should have told you, Patty, but..."

"Yes, I imagine you *should have*, Dad! Now look what you've caused."

"Mommie! You don't understand. The angel said we have to find Ole Pa's magic tree!"

What could she mean, *find the magic tree?* I had not said anything to Jenny about a tree—not that I could recall. Although surely I must have. But I'd already confirmed that the tree was no longer there, so this could not end well.

Patty looked at me and frowned. "Dad, what is this about a *magic tree*? Have you been filling her head with some silly superstition?"

"No Patty, I—I don't know how she could know about—I mean, I've not said anything to her about . . ."

"Dad, what's going on here?"

"Well, there was this tree. . .I mean, when I was a little boy. It was across the road from where we lived. I just sort of thought of it as my special tree...you know how kids think certain things have magic powers. But, well, I'm afraid it's not there anymore. Now there's just a playground, with some swings and ball fields. There are no trees at all anymore. I'm sorry...but I can't understand how Jenny could know about the tree? I'm pretty sure I never said anything to her—or to anyone else—about that tree. And like I said, there aren't any trees there anymore, anyway."

"Yes, there *are*, Ole Pa! And we have to go and find it! The angel said so!"

I glanced at Patty. "Well, I guess it can't hurt just to drive by again." Turning to Jenny, I said, "I bet Mommy would like to see you swing like we did the other day, okay Jenny?"

"Okay, but first we have to find the tree, Ole Pa!"

"I'm sorry, Jenny...didn't you see when we were there before that there are no trees anymore?"

"You'll see," Jenny said, rolling her eyes. "Angels DON'T lie!"

I drove on; what choice did I have?

By the time I turned and headed down the familiar street, I again started asking myself the same questions. Why was Jenny so determined to come back here? How could she possibly know about the tree? An angel had told her? No, obviously I must have said something about the tree sometime and had simply forgotten. I was almost certain that he never had, though. Clara Wilson had mentioned an angel in her notes. Could that be to what Jenny was referring now?

Patty was staring strangely at me, almost as if she thought I was crazy. *Crazy*, well I guessed I would have to agreed. *That must be it*, I decided. *I'm going crazy—or I've already gone—just like the old woman. Maybe some of her craziness rubbed off.*

As we rounded the curve near where my old house had been and approached the playground, Jenny yelled, "Ole Pa, stop! Stop here!"

Pulling off the road, I stopped directly in front of one of the softball fields. As I got out of the car, I felt something tugging at my heart. Uncertain what to expect, I slowly unfolded the little wheelchair. Then Patty and I helped Jenny into the chair and I began pushing her across the ball field. Heading generally in the direction of the swings, I hoped maybe we could just push Jenny in the swings for a while, and then go home.

When we neared where second base should be, I stopped and looked back across the street, toward the site of my old house. I found himself trying to get a bearing on where the tree had once stood—not that it mattered now, of course. I decided it must have been somewhere near where we were now standing, although I couldn't be certain. Perhaps it was somewhere to our left, I decided, and without thinking, turned and began pushing the wheelchair toward the third base line.

"Ole Pa!" Jenny shouted. "You're going the wrong way!"

"The wrong way?"

"Yes! Turn around! Go that way," she directed, pointing back across the field toward the first base line.

How could Jenny know this, I again wondered, as I turned and pushed the wheelchair back across the infield.

As we drew near the first base line, Jenny pointed out toward right field and directed, "It's out there! Go that way!"

Patty and I looked across the outfield but could see nothing except some overgrown grass that needed mowing before the softball season began. The chair quickly became difficult to push through the deep grass, but just as I was about to turn around and go back, I noticed something. It looked like a small patch of grass, which appeared somewhat taller than the surrounding grass. I stopped and rubbed my eyes. Patty stared in the direction I was looking and flashed me a questioning frown. I shrugged.

"Go, Ole Pa! Faster! Don't you see it?" Jenny screamed. Suddenly the chair seemed to become easier to push, almost as if something were drawing it in that direction.

"Ole Pa! Mommy! There it is! See, I told you!" Jenny exclaimed, pointing to what appeared to be a patch of taller grass, or possibly weeds.

"There *what* is, Jenny?" asked Patty.

"I'm afraid it's just some weeds, Jenny," I said. "I don't want you to be disappointed. What if we just go swing for a few—"

"Ole Pa! Can't you see it? It's right there, right where the angel said it would be!"

I felt my heartbeat quicken and began to experience a sensation I had not felt for a long time. I was afraid to acknowledge what might be happening here—what surely *must* be happening. It couldn't be possible—could it?

Suddenly I realized that this taller patch of grass might not be grass at all. Instead, it looked more like a small plant that had somehow pushed its way above the top of the grass.

"It's just a weed, Jenny," I argued weakly, more in an effort to convince myself than Jenny. "How about we push you in the swings and then we'll go, okay?"

"No! No, Ole Pa! Keep going. It's the *tree*! Don't you see it? It's the magic tree, just like the angel said."

My heart pounded. How could Jenny possibly know about a magic tree? And why was she so excited? There was no tree here now. Yet, as I looked again, I imagined I saw the plant's tiny leaves beckoning me closer. Blinking my eyes, I looked again. The leaves continued to wave in the wind and I felt a stronger urge to hurry toward it. Glancing at Patty, I could sense that she felt something too.

As we drew nearer, I noticed that it did look sort of like a tiny tree. Could it be a baby sugar maple, I wondered, remembering how the wind blew the seeds across the field. Could this be a small tree that had finally come up, even after the big trees had all been cut down? Could it actually be a descendent of my magic tree? This had to be a little sugar maple tree, I decided, since I knew of no other tree with a five-pointed, twin-leaf arrangement such as what I was now seeing. This little tree was hardly more than eighteen inches tall, yet it looked almost like a miniature version of a full-grown tree.

When we were close enough for me to see more clearly, I was even more amazed. Except for its size, this tiny tree looked almost exactly like a miniature version of the large tree I remembered from so long ago. Seeing it now reminded me of how I had pictured my special tree in my mind all these years. For some reason, I began trying to recall what they called those small trees the Japanese grew. *Bonsai* trees, I suddenly remembered. This must be sort of like a Bonsai tree. Then I began to comprehend that this *was* actually a tiny maple tree. . .a sugar maple to be exact.

As I pushed the chair closer, I began to experience those same feelings I remembered from so many years ago. Could this possibly be *my* tree? No, of course not! Yet, might it be a *child* of my tree—or perhaps a *grandchild*?

"Ole Pa! Mommy! Look! See, I told you. It's the magic tree!"

Tears welled up in my eyes as I pushed the little wheelchair close enough for Jenny to touch the tiny tree. Reaching out, she brushed the leaves with her fingertips, then she reached down and placed her fingers against the small tree trunk. When she withdrew her hand, she brought it to her mouth and touched her fingers lightly to her lips. Patty and I then watched in amazement as a look of joy spread across the little girl's face. Had she perhaps tasted the sweet sap of the sugar maple tree?

Suddenly, without warning, Jenny stood.

Patty gasped, grabbed my arm and we watched, mesmerized, as Jenny slowly turned loose of her wheelchair. Then, before we could believe it was happening, she took an unassisted step, her first since the accident. Then another. . .and another.

I stared at the little tree and imagined I saw its tiny leaves turning upward toward the sky, almost as if smiling. I looked at Patty and tears flooded both our eyes as we watched Jenny stride around the tree, her legs seeming to become stronger with each step. First she walked slowly, then she began to run, circling the tree repeatedly, giggling, running faster, her arms over her head, as if reaching for the stars.

"Mommy, look! I can run again!"

Patty wiped her eyes. "Yes, sweetie, I see. I'm so happy!" Patty grabbed my arm and began to giggle along with the little girl. Then we hugged as we continued to laugh and cry at the same time.

Jenny suddenly stopped, came over to her mother and looked up with a questioning expression. "This doesn't mean we have to go back, does it Mommy? I don't ever wanna go back there. I just wanna stay here forever. Please, Mommy. We don't have to go back now, do we?"

"No, sweetheart," Patty said, tears again flooding her eyes. "It doesn't mean that at all." Patty glanced at me and added, "I think we'll be staying here for a long, long time. Maybe it's time you got back in school; what'd you think, sweetie?"

"Okay, Mommy. I'm ready!"

Jenny reached out and again brushed the tiny leaves with her fingertips, then she bent down and kissed the top of the tiny tree. She stood just for a moment, looking reverently at the little tree, then brushing the leaves once more with her fingertips, she turned and ran toward the swings. Patty and I each gently touched the small treetop, and then we turned and followed the giggling little girl across the field, leaving the wheelchair sitting beside the tree.

After we had walked a few paces, I felt compelled to stop. Without knowing why, I turned and looked back over my shoulder across the field.

"Patty, look!"

"What?" asked Patty, turning to look in the direction he was staring.

"Back there in the field! Do you see anything?"

"No, I..."

I could tell by her expression that Patty didn't see the tree, either. Suddenly, it appeared that nothing but tall grass was growing in the field—there was no tree at all. Had there ever been? Had we all just imagined this whole thing? Then suddenly I realized something else, something even more remarkable...unbelievable. Where was the wheelchair? Jenny's wheelchair seemed also to have disappeared. I looked at Patty and we stood, shaking our heads. This could not be real; surely it must all be a dream.

Patty and I stood for a long time just watching the happy little girl as she swung higher and higher, giggling, pushing with her feet, pumping, her legs already seeming as good as new. Then through my tears, I again looked back across the field, but as before, all I saw now was tall grass. Then, for some reason, I slowly raised my eyes skyward. It had to be an illusion, some trick of lighting, of course...but there, floating high overhead was what appeared to be a tiny wheelchair, just disappearing into the clouds. Squinting into the bright sunlight, I strained to see better, but now I could not see anything unusual. Noticing my gaze, Patty looked up, but all either of us could see now were a few odd-shaped clouds drifting lazily across the deep blue sky.

Jenny giggled as she continued to swing higher and higher, bringing us quickly back to reality...or at least to the understanding that what we were seeing now somehow had to be real...our little girl had been magically transformed back to the Jenny of old, the *walking, running, happy* Jenny. How it had happened? Perhaps we would never know.

Smiling, I allowed mind to drift back to my boyhood, back to my *tree* from so long ago. How could I any longer deny that it had been real? There could no longer be any question that the magic of believing could create miracles.

Later that evening, as I lay in bed reliving the miraculous experience, a sudden inspiration came upon me. Strangely, the theme of my next novel slowly manifested itself into my consciousness. Somehow, I knew now that I was ready to write my book, and he also knew what the title would be: *The Fixing Tree.*